♦*DREAMING OF A WHITE CHIRSTMAS*♦

Hollywood Legends Book Five

Mary J. Williams

© 2016

TABLE OF CONTENTS

ABOUT THE AUTHOR

Writing isn't easy. But I love every second. A blank screen isn't the enemy. It is the opportunity to create new friends and take them on amazing adventures and life-changing journeys. I feel blessed to spend my days weaving tales that are unique—because I made them.

Billionaires. Songwriters. Artists. Actors. Directors. Stuntmen. Football players. They fill the pages and become dear friends I hope you will want to revisit again and again.

Thank you for jumping into my books and coming along for the journey.

HOW TO GET IN TOUCH

Please visit me at these sites, sign up for my newsletter or leave a message.

http://www.maryjwilliams.net/

https://www.facebook.com/maryjwilliamsauthor/?ref=hl

https://twitter.com/maryjwilliams05

https://www.pinterest.com/maryj0675/

https://www.instagram.com/2015romance/

https://www.goodreads.com/author/show/5648619.Mary_J_Williams

MORE BOOKS BY MARY J. WILLIAMS

Harper Falls Series
If I Loved You

If Tomorrow Never Comes

If You Only Knew

If I Had You (Christmas in Harper Falls)

Hollywood Legends Series
Dreaming with a Broken Heart

Dreaming with My Eyes Wide Open

Dreaming of Your Love

Dreaming Again

One Pass Away Series
After the Rain

After All These Years

After the Fire

Hart of Rock and Roll
Flowers on the Wall

Flowers and Cages

Flowers are Red

Flowers for Zoe (Coming in December)

PROLOGUE

ON A LATE December afternoon, watching the snow fall was simply magical. The warm, cozy house smelled of baking cookies and freshly cut pine boughs. In the corner of the room, a fifteen-foot Blue Spruce stood, all sparkling lights, glittery garlands of tinsel and loaded with antique ornaments handed down from generation to generation. New decorations were added each year celebrating additions to the family.

Callie Flynn stood by the tree. They weren't spending the holiday in their Beverly Hills house. They were at a ranch in Montana owned by a dear old friend, Chuck Chamberlin. Still, it felt like home. Chuck's daughter was married to Callie's son, making them family *and* friends. The best of both worlds.

With care, Callie placed her contributions on the already loaded branches. The first were for her boys—Wyatt, Garrett, Nathaniel, and Colton. Handmade in blue and ivory, they had been gifts from her husband, a raised initial in the center. The memories of those early Christmas mornings brought a lump to Callie's throat, a bit of moisture forming in her famous, changeable eyes. At the moment, they sparkled like pure silver. Bright and alive with emotion.

She was a woman with many facets. The world knew and adored the award-winning actress. Fast approaching sixty, neither her mirror nor the motion picture camera showed her age. Up close, with little makeup, Callie Flynn was the true definition of an ageless beauty. Genetics helped. She watched her diet and hit the gym—and the yoga mat—regularly. Moisturizer was the one beauty product she refused to live without.

Everyone wanted to know her secret. What was Callie Flynn's fountain of youth? Why did she defy time and Mother Nature when others gave into the lure of cosmetic procedures that left them looking more frightful than youthful?

When asked, Callie never hesitated. It wasn't a secret. One couldn't find it in a bottle or under the surgeon's knife. It didn't involve extracts from the Amazon or secretions from the backside of a rare two-toned Himalayan Yak.

It was a one-word answer. Simple, but not as easy to find as one might think. Happiness.

The front door burst open with a swirl of cold air and snow. Following close behind, the sound that made Callie smile. The warmth of her family's laughter.

4

The four women, bundled up for a walk around the ranch, stomped their feet before entering. Beaming at the sight, Callie sighed. They weren't biologically hers, but they belonged to her nonetheless. The daughters of her heart if not her body.

Flame-haired Jade. Once so fragile, now fierce as they came. She and Garrett were a perfect match. Paige, a blond beauty with the heart of a lion. Her sweetness that won over Nathaniel, the tough-as-nails stuntman with a marshmallow center.

Then there was Sable. Ex-Army Ranger, she was hired as a bodyguard to protect Callie's youngest, winning Colton's love along the way. And finally Joie. Smart and funny, she was the perfect balm for a wounded soul. It was a lucky day indeed when Wyatt, the oldest Landis boy, met her. She showed him the possibilities. He deserved to be happy. That love—honest and true—was possible.

"Where are your men?" Callie asked, greeting them with hugs.

"Out being manly," Paige laughed as she hung up her coat. "Dad loaded them, Caleb, and a bunch of feed into the old Ford. They are headed out to feed the cattle in the south field."

"No women allowed." Sable ran her fingers through her short cap of dark hair, her smile indulgent. "I had to remind Colton that he isn't a rancher. He only played one in the movies."

"There is hot chocolate on the stove," Callie told them, holding out a basket for them to deposit their damp gloves.

"That sounds like heaven. Junior has a sweet tooth." Paige rubbed her barely discernible baby bump. The ultrasound had determined grandchild number three would be another irresistible Landis boy. Women of the world beware. "I try to convince him that spinach is better, but all he wants is cookies. And cake. Oh, is there any cake?"

"It was the same when I was pregnant with his father. If given a choice, Nate would have lived on chocolate twenty-four hours a day. I swear his first word was Hershey." Laughing, Callie put an arm around Paige's growing waistline. "As for the cake, there may be a piece tucked away in the pantry."

"You are the best mother-in-law ever." Paige would have said that no matter what. She loved Callie. However, the promise of frosting-laden pastry made her want to do a jig.

"Save me some hot chocolate," Joie said as she hung up her coat. "I need to check on my little angel."

The words were said with love—Joie's tongue firmly planted in her cheek. Though she had just turned two, Francesca Landis believed the world revolved around her. And she wasn't far off base. As the first grandchild—and a girl—the doting had begun the second she let out her first red-faced squall. She had her father's determination and her mother's creativity. The combination could be a handful. She was the center of attention—and loved every second.

Joie had worried what would happen when another baby inevitably came along. Last month after Jade gave birth, the family held their collective breaths. It turned out Francesca had inherited more than her grandmother's famous gray eyes. She was blessed with Callie's big heart. She couldn't get enough of her cousin, declaring with all seriousness that Aaron was *her* baby.

"She was perfect. As usual." Callie didn't mention that it took two stories and a promise of two more this afternoon before the little girl would agree to take a nap. Nothing new. Francesca already possessed her grandfather's knack for negotiating a deal.

"I hope Aaron is ready for his mid-day meal. My breasts feel like they are ready to burst." Jade groaned when the button on her shirt popped open. "The men in my life might like the size of these puppies. I'm not a fan."

"I can tell you from experience," Callie brushed her hand over Jade's hair. "When you are ready to stop nursing, and your breasts go back to their normal size, Garrett will be just as happy."

"Because he loves me." Jade remembered a time when she hadn't thought it possible to find a man like Garrett—or to be this happy. "You raised an amazing man, Callie."

"Amen," Joie agreed.

"I have no complaints about mine," Sable laughed.

"Make that a perfect four," Paige nodded. Then after a little thought added a qualifier. "Maybe not perfect. How boring would that be? But so close I would be a fool to complain."

As Jade and Joie went off to check on the children, Callie took five mugs from the cupboard, her heart full of so much love and thankfulness she wondered how it stayed in her chest. Paige was right, their lives were not perfect.

The Landis clan was considered Hollywood royalty. However, they dealt with the joys and tragedies any family encountered, along with the arguments and misunderstandings. It was how they dealt with the bad that made the good so much better. If one person had a problem, there was always somebody to help find a solution. Callie watched with pride as her sons grew up as brothers *and* best friends. Something that had never changed.

"Gam!"

The giggling shout came from the wiggling bundle in Joie's arms. Giving her daughter a kiss, she set Francesca down a few feet from Callie. The little girl liked to get a running start—wherever her destination.

"A few minutes ago, *I* was all she cared about. Then she turned her affections to Aaron. Now it's Grandma. So fickle."

"It's all about love, isn't it, sweetheart?" Callie lifted Francesca onto her lap, cuddling her close. The little arms went around her neck without hesitation. So much unadulterated affection.

"Wuv, Gam. Wuv, Ma. Wuv, Da. Wuv, wuv, wuv," Francesca chanted, her face glowing.

Callie held her granddaughter, content to watch the activity around her. Paige turned on some music, the soft strains of Christmas carols adding the perfect backdrop. So many holidays. So many happy memories.

Taking a deep breath, Callie let her mind drift back in time. She rarely dealt in what ifs. It was a futile exercise. However, she couldn't help thinking about the life she might have lived. There was a time when she had thought she would never marry. Never have children. She had been focused on her career, with no time for anything else.

Luckily for Callie, a big, handsome man named Caleb Landis came along. Not that he was looking for a lifetime commitment. From the moment he saw her, Caleb wanted Callie Flynn. The rest—the life they built together—came later. Thank God.

Callie rested her hand on the arm of her darling Francesca, who, for the moment, was content to sit on Grandma's lap, munching on a brightly decorated cookie. She smiled, thinking of her sons, their wives, and all the love stories she had been witness to over the last few years.

Smiling, she thought of another time. Before cell phones and email. When it was impossible to imagine texting a message or tweeting one's thoughts. Instagram or Snapchat? Nope. In those days, it took more effort to track somebody down. Asking them out meant talking in person or—God forbid—on a landline. Not exactly prehistoric, but today's young people might think so.

Closing her eyes, Callie's mind drifted back thirty-six years. To when she met Caleb. To the love story that started it all..

CHAPTER ONE

HOLLYWOOD—1980

"PULL YOUR HEAD out of your back side, Simon. It's time movies reflected that this is a new decade—the last part of the twentieth century. Women need to be portrayed as more than victims or braless bimbos."

Few people spoke to Simon Wendt that way. He started producing movies before Callie was born. They weren't the classiest films, but they made a ton of money. In Hollywood, that made him a very important man.

"This is an action flick, Callie. Audiences come to see two things. Explosions and bare breasts." Simon snickered—loudly—drawing the attention of several diners. The restaurant was a Hollywood hotspot for doing business. "I guess technically that makes three things."

Ignoring the lame joke, Callie didn't crack a smile, her gray eyes going from cool to stormy. "Not *my* breasts."

"If you want this part, you better be willing to lose your top—*and* your attitude."

At times, Callie wished she had never left Iowa. Things were simpler there. *Which is why you left*, she reminded herself. Callie's dreams of fame and fortune started early. They didn't mesh with the life she would have led if she followed the path of so many of her friends.

Two years ago, Callie could have married her high school sweetheart. He asked. Because she genuinely liked him and didn't want to sound ungrateful, she pretended to think about it. Then, as gently as possible, she said no. Three days later, she was on a bus for Los Angeles. Callie Flynn was born in a small town, but she had always been a big-city girl at heart. From the time she was old enough to get a job, Callie had saved every dime. It wasn't a lot, but enough to get her on her way.

Finding work wasn't difficult. Callie began waiting tables within a week. She found an apartment to share with three other aspiring actresses. It was cheap, and the bus line ran right outside the door. She spent her spare time taking acting classes, searching for reputable representation, and going to every open casting call that she could find.

It was at one of these—a year after leaving Iowa—where Callie caught her first break. The part was in a small, independent film. Originally meant to be one line, the director was so impressed by Callie's reading, he cast her in a different, showier part. The movie hadn't exactly rocked the world. Not even a minor tremor. However, Callie made a minor splash. Enough to get her an interview with a high-powered agent.

Two movies later—each a little bigger and better than the last—Callie found herself with a chance to co-star alongside the current box office golden boy in a film that would up her profile a thousand times over.

"That's it?" Callie couldn't believe there was no middle ground. "I go topless, or I'm out?"

"Honey, you were never in. Actresses are a dime a dozen in this town. Interchangeable," Simon informed her with a sneer. Snapping his fingers, he ordered a double scotch on the rocks. "You could wear a paper bag over your head for all the audience would care. Tits and ass are what they're looking for. I admit yours *are* prime."

Callie felt her skin crawl as Simon looked her up and down. She knew what was coming. She had dealt with the proverbial casting couch on multiple occasions. However, it never failed to make her sorry that so many men insisted on deteriorating into a big, fat Hollywood cliché.

"Why don't we move this discussion to my office?"

Cliché on top of cliché. Simon's *office*? Callie didn't even rate a sleazy hotel room? She didn't know if Simon were cheap or it was a reflection on her. Not that it mattered. This interview was over.

"Let me save you the embarrassment. I'm not interested in doing you *or* your movie."

Simon looked around. Callie hadn't raised her voice, but the proximity of the tables made it impossible for those closest to have missed the exchange. His face reddened when he heard the undisguised laughter. Oops. It seemed she *hadn't* saved embarrassing him.

"You have made a huge mistake," Simon warned.

Callie Flynn tossed her long, sun-streaked brown hair over her shoulder. With the dignity of a queen, and knowing she might have burned a very important bridge, she rose without a word. She turned on her heel, causing the

10

skirt of the dress that cost more than she could afford, to swirl around her legs. Nobody looking could tell she felt like vomiting or that her insides shook worse than her mother's prized raspberry jelly during an earthquake.

Keeping her expression neutral and her emotions at bay might have been the best performance of Callie's very young career.

CALEB LANDIS WATCHED the gorgeous brunette exit the restaurant. Intrigued wasn't the right word for his reaction. Something about the young woman had drawn his eye the moment he entered the restaurant. When he noticed who she was with, his interest hadn't waned; he simply waited to see how things played out.

Through Caleb's lunch with his assistant, he watched the play of emotions over the lady's face. If she wasn't an actress, she should be. Her range was amazing. With the right script and director, there was no telling how great she could be. And those eyes. From where he sat, he could see the different shades of gray. Cool to stormy, they told a story all by themselves.

The more Caleb watched, the more he knew she would be perfect for the movie he had in production. When she let Simon Wendt have it with both barrels, Caleb smiled. *That* was a woman he had to know.

"Go back to the office. I'll see you later."

"Where are you going?" Nadine Black put her pad and paper into the satchel that sat at her feet. Five years ago, Caleb had hired her fresh out of secretarial school. Efficient, smarter than was sometimes comfortable, and unwaveringly loyal, it was one of the best decisions he ever made. His career had taken off soon after. Caleb didn't think the timing was a coincidence. Making movies was a stressful business. Knowing he could trust Nadine to keep the office running smoothly gave him the freedom to concentrate on other things.

Right now, Caleb's mind was on a pair of long, sexy legs as they exited the restaurant.

"I need to speak with Simon Wendt."

"Why?" Nadine asked with amazement.

"Call it professional courtesy."

Without giving Nadine a chance to respond, Caleb crossed the room to where Simon bucked up his wounded ego with another glass of scotch. It was no secret that Caleb considered Wendt to be—at best—a sleaze ball schlock master. Caleb wasn't one of those in Hollywood who kowtowed to the man because he made money—a lot of money. He believed movies could be successful without always playing to the lowest common denominator. A fact he proved with his last three films.

They attended many of the same parties. It was important to know who had the money. Without investors, movies did not get made. Caleb and Simon Wendt often vied against each other. Lately, Caleb came out the winner more often than not. He and Wendt had barely exchanged five words. They would never be colleagues. However, this was Hollywood. Caleb Landis had established himself as a major player. That meant when he approached Simon's table, the other man shook his hand like he was a long-lost friend. Like the piece of hair Wendt sported on the top of his head, the greeting was fake and poorly executed.

"Landis," Simon held onto Caleb's hand a few shakes too long. "It's been awhile. Sit. How about something to drink?"

"Not for me, thank you." Caleb smiled at the waitress when Simon signaled her over. She smiled back, hitching her hip in a provocative manner. She was cute, but he wasn't interested.

"You heard the man." Simon shooed the waitress away.

"I don't want to keep you." The truth was, Caleb wanted to spend as little time in the man's company as possible. He could have gotten the information he sought from a different source. But he was curious why the woman had been with Wendt.

"Not a problem. My date was called away unexpectedly. I thought she would be filling my afternoon—if you know what I mean." Wendt drained what was left of his drink. "What can I do for you?"

"The woman that was with you? Is she an actress?"

"That's what she calls herself." Wendt sneered, rattling the ice in his empty glass. "I was going to help her out by giving her a part in my next movie. Can you believe the bimbo turned me down because of a bit of tasteful nudity? She'll be back on the farm in six months. Or turning tricks down on the strip. A little talent can take her only so far. She's unwilling to cooperate. Bye, bye, Callie Flynn."

"Callie Flynn." Caleb rolled the name around in his head. It was a good name. "Who's representing her?"

"Millicent Fitzhugh. Is that what this is about?" Wendt cackled, slapping the table. "You think you're going to sleep with her? Good luck."

Caleb didn't correct Simon Wendt. He was attracted to the beautiful actress. But his motivation had nothing to do with getting her into bed. With the talent he instinctively knew she possessed, she would take him another rung up the Hollywood ladder.

In return, Caleb would make Callie Flynn a star.

"YOU SLY PUSS."

Storm McIntosh, one of Callie's roommates, met her at the door. The petite blonde saw every woman as a threat. Whether it was an acting job or a man, she was always ready to push the competition under the bus. Callie had tried to be friendly, but Storm made it clear she wasn't interested in anybody who couldn't advance her career. Callie definitely did not qualify.

Callie's feet were killing her from a double shift at the diner. On top of the disastrous meeting with Simon Wendt, she was about as low as she could remember. She wanted a hot shower before sinking into oblivion for the next eight hours. Storm never had a good word to say. Most of the time, Callie ignored the woman's less-than-subtle jabs. Tonight, she wasn't in the mood.

"Whatever it is, keep it to yourself."

"I would, but Jules was the one who took the message. She had to leave for work and asked me to tell you."

In other words, if Storm had answered the phone, Callie would never have known about the call. The answering machine was communal. Whoever came home first was supposed to write everything down and pass it along. Jules had missed an important audition because Storm accidentally forgot to tell her. They would have kicked the bitch out long ago if her name wasn't on the lease. Callie had been looking for a new place, but they weren't easy to come by. For now, she tried to avoid the woman whenever possible.

"Okay," Callie sighed. She was so tired of Storm's games. "Should I wait for Jules, or are you going to give me the message?"

Apparently disappointed that Callie refused to jump through her hoops, Storm shrugged.

"Your agent called. It seems you have caught the eye of Caleb Landis." When Callie didn't respond, Storm slowed her speech as if she were talking to a slow-witted child. "Caleb Landis. Tall. Gorgeous. The kind of man nobody says no to. I wouldn't. He could do his worst, and I would say, *please, sir. I want some more.*"

Leave it to her roommate to turn a Dickens quote into something dirty. Ignoring Storm, Callie casually walked to the bathroom. Closing the door, she looked into the cracked mirror over the sink, taking a deep breath. Caleb Landis? Holy crap. Callie did a quick jig around the tiny room before gripping the sink so hard her knuckles turned white.

Callie knew about Caleb Landis, and it had nothing to do with his looks. He was a young producer who had established a reputation for quality movies that the public wanted to see. Not an easy task these days. His last production, *Time Ran Out*, was the best film she had seen in years. She watched enraptured, totally immersed in the story. Then spent the next week envying the actress who played the lead. It was exactly the kind of part Callie longed for. She knew it was above her reach at the moment.

Someday, she promised herself, an aspiring actress would sit in a darkened theater, green to the gills, wanting to be Callie Flynn.

For now, Callie was ready for that next step. She stripped off her waitress uniform, looking forward to the time when she could toss the blue and white polyester into the trash. She thought about burning the offending garment but was afraid the fumes from whatever was added to the fabric to make it almost indestructible, would cause a health hazard for anybody in a five-mile radius.

Chuckling at the foolish way her mind sometimes worked, Callie turned the shower on full blast. In the case of the apartment's ancient plumbing, that meant little more than a sad trickle. Having washed her hair that morning, Callie was able to simply stand under the water and pretend it sprayed her body with more power than a child's squirt gun.

Five minutes later, Callie had dried herself off, donned her favorite silk-like robe and crossed her fingers that Storm had left the apartment. Or at the very least, disappeared into her bedroom.

Luck was on Callie's side. The living room with its third and fourth-hand furniture was unoccupied. Sitting on the faded sofa with the patched up holes— carefully avoiding the spring that always popped through the middle cushion, Callie picked up the phone and dialed. After the usual delay getting rerouted from the switchboard to Millicent's secretary, she finally had her agent on the line.

"Callie." Millicent never bothered with incidental chit chat. Look up *time is money* in the dictionary and one would find the woman's picture. "How did it go with Simon Wendt?"

"It didn't. Or rather, I wouldn't sleep with him to get a crappy part that consisted of me cowering in one corner after another—topless."

"This business is crowded with male sleazebags, honey. And more than a few females of the same ilk." Callie could see Millicent, her feet on her desk, her expression pragmatic. "You were never an innocent from the sticks with starlight in her eyes. That's one of the reasons I know you're going to make it in Hollywood. Simon Wendt won't send you rushing back to Ohio with your tail between your legs."

"Iowa." Callie laughed. Millicent never got it right because she didn't care. Los Angeles, California was her home, Hollywood the center of her universe. The rest of the world might as well not exist.

"For some reason, you say that with pride." There was amazed exasperation in Millicent's voice. "Forget about corn country. Forget about Simon Wendt. You are on the cusp of the big time."

"Caleb Landis." Just saying the name of such a quality producer made Callie's heart jump.

"He's the real deal. No casting couch allowed."

Callie hadn't realized she was holding her breath. Slowly—with relief—she let it out.

"I need details, Millicent. When did he call? What's the project? How big is the part? Is there a meeting? A cold reading? A screen test? Where—"

"Slow down, motor mouth. You're getting ahead of everybody."

Millicent didn't understand. Callie felt like she was running behind—constantly trying to catch up. She had a birthday six months ago. Twenty years old. Young in most people's eyes. But a woman in Hollywood faced a different reality. As one nasty—but unfortunately accurate—director once likened a woman's aging to a dog's. One year was like seven. Callie wanted to throw her drink in the asshole's face. She might have if it would have changed anything.

The fact was, actors like Paul Newman and Sean Connery were treated like fine wine. They aged, the movie-going public continued to swoon. With very few exceptions, women had the shelf life of a peach. As soon as a wrinkle or two began to show, they were delegated to the trash heap. Easily tossed away, quickly forgotten.

In her head, Callie knew she had plenty of years left. However, with each one that passed, her chances of a long, lasting career diminished. *Now* was her time to make a splash. She felt it in her bones.

"Tell me what I need to do, Millicent." The hunger in Callie's voice vibrated around the room, through the phone, and into her agent's ear. "Short of giving him my body, Caleb Landis can have anything he wants. I would offer him my first born except—"

"I know," Millicent laughed, having heard it more than once. "Your career is your life. No marriage. No children. Honey, you're a baby. It's likely you'll change your mind."

"You didn't."

"Me? I was an old war horse at birth," Millicent said, her tone showing not an ounce of regret. "You, on the other hand, have just the right amount of grit and toughness. But your heart isn't hardened. Mark my words, the right man—at the right moment—will change your mind."

Callie didn't argue. Why bother? *She* knew the truth. Spouses and children needed time and attention. On a good day, Callie could barely sneak in a shower and a good night's sleep. Unless she could find a stay-at-home husband who was capable of miraculously giving birth, she planned to devote her life to one thing—becoming the best and hardest working actress on the planet.

"First things first," Callie said, effectively turning the subject away from her personal life. "Tell me what Caleb Landis wants."

CHAPTER TWO

"I WANT AN actress who can be vulnerable one second, a crazed protector the next, with an occasional glimpse of romantic and sexy."

"Then you want me."

Callie barely contained a gasp as Caleb's eyes met hers, the blue depths blazing with passion. Not toward her. He was all about the movie. From the moment they shook hands, Caleb Landis had been charming yet professional. Sexy yet non-threatening. Tall, broad-shouldered, his suit was tailored perfectly to fit his trim body. Under different circumstances, Callie could imagine pursuing the tingle of attraction.

Caleb gave Callie the impression he might be interested in her as a woman. However, not once did he say or do anything that made her uncomfortable. He was the producer. She was the actress. They were meeting in his office. Not once was the line between producer and actress crossed—not even close.

Millicent had assured her that Caleb Landis didn't operate that way. He didn't get involved with actresses. Not ones he worked with. According to the gossip rags, the women he dated were an interesting hodgepodge. Lawyers, athletes, models. Occasionally he dipped into the thespian pool. But never somebody currently in his employ. It was a hard and fast rule. One he never broke.

"I appreciate confidence, Ms. Flynn."

"Callie."

Caleb nodded. "We couldn't be speaking if I didn't think you were the right woman for the part. I screened your last two films. The potential is there, lying just beneath the surface. The question is, can you tap into those hidden depths when you need to?"

Callie had complete faith in her abilities. The directors she worked with seemed happy with the performances she gave them. Caleb asked for more. Something both scary and exhilarating. She told him she could do it, but what if she *didn't* have it in her? *No*, she admonished herself. *This is the chance you've been dreaming about. Failure is not an option.*

"Lying to you would be foolish, Mr. Landis."

"Caleb," he teased lightly.

Callie smiled, relaxing into her chair. "I don't have a lot of acting experience, Caleb. I'm young. You would be taking a big chance if you gave me this part. But I read the script. *Meant to Be* is brilliant. I understand the part. I can bring the character of Tessa to life."

Caleb sat back, his gaze locked with hers. Hands clasped, he tapped one long finger against his chin as if taking the measure of her and her words.

"My director wants to meet with you. Are you familiar with T.K. Paulson?"

Was he kidding? The most casual movie-goer knew T.K. Paulson's work. He was one of those rare directors able to seamlessly straddle all genres. His action movies drew adoring crowds. His romantic comedies brought out the laughs, tears, and tissues. The last film he directed garnered him an Oscar nomination.

When Callie was alone in her cramped bedroom—the one she shared with the messiest roommate on the face of the Earth—she planned on hitting her knees, giving thanks to God, Allah, Shiva, and every other deity she could bring to mind. Somebody was watching out for her. Whoever. Whatever. She didn't care. She wanted them to know she appreciated the boost.

"Tell me the time and place. I'll be there," Callie replied calmly. Not bad for a woman whose insides were jumping and popping like a drop of water on a scalding hot cast-iron skillet.

"How about now?"

"Now?" Callie swallowed. "Sure. That would be great."

Holy crap, holy crap, holy crap. Things were happening fast. Callie stared hard at Caleb's poker face. Was this a test? The Hollywood equivalent of a pop quiz? Well, bring it on, Mr. Producer. She had her foot in the door. There was no way she would let anything trip her up now.

Nodding, Caleb pushed the intercom button.

"Nadine? Is T.K. still out there hanging on your every word?"

"Fuck you, Landis," a smoke-roughened voice shot back.

"Charming," Caleb chuckled. "Leave my assistant alone and get in here."

"Why would I do that?"

18

Caleb took his finger off the button. "The man is a brilliant director. Once he moves from behind the camera, his mind is like a sieve. It doesn't help that he's been trying for months to get Nadine to agree to go out with him. Wisely, she keeps turning him down. I promise you, Callie. T.K. knows you're waiting to meet him. By now, Nadine has dropped a less-than-subtle reminder."

"Damn it," T.K. shouted, bursting through the office door. "Why didn't you just say she was in here? Does making me feel like an ass give you some kind of perverted pleasure?"

"Yes. But there's nothing perverted about it."

"So you say," T.K. grinned, giving Caleb a friendly slap on the back.

Shorter, slighter, with a mop of unruly black hair and a scruffy beard, T.K. Paulson didn't have Caleb's physical presence. In a crowded room, he would blend into the woodwork while Caleb would stand out, drawing all eyes with his good looks and charisma. However, the minute T.K. shook Callie's hand and began to speak, she knew why actors loved working with him. He knew how to communicate his vision of the movie.

What Callie thought would be more of a meet and greet, quickly evolved into something much more. Never shy about giving her opinion, she jumped in with how she interpreted the text of the script and what she read beneath the surface. T.K. fired back with a series of probing questions. Now and then, Caleb would inject a comment, but for the most part, he let the director and Callie exchange ideas without interruption.

By the time T.K. asked Callie to read a scene, she was comfortable— warmed up from their lively discussion. Her nerves had fallen away.

"Which scene would you like me to do?"

"Tessa's monologue toward the end of the script." T.K. flipped through his copy. "Page—"

"I know the one you mean." Callie breathed deeply. She centered her thoughts, finding the character that she already knew so well. When she raised her eyes, the shade of gray was mellow and serene. "Okay. I'm ready."

Caleb and T.K. exchanged surprised looks.

"Don't you want a copy of the script to read?"

Callie shrugged, her smile self-deprecating. "I inhaled every word the second I got my hands on the pages. For the past week, I've lived Tessa's journey over and over. In bed. In the shower. At work. I know the words by heart."

A shadow passed across Caleb's face. Disappointment, Callie thought. She knew what he was thinking. She was another actress who thought she could get away with reciting the words by rote. He had hoped she would make the words her own instead of simply spewing them out.

Caleb's reaction didn't bother Callie. He barely knew her. One meeting and a screening of her movies weren't enough information. *Soon*, she thought, taking another breath. Either he would understand who she was as an actress or she was about to fall flat on her face. The hell with that. Callie's resolve strengthened. This was her chance. If she had to, she would use the sheer force of her will to make Caleb understand she was the only actress capable of playing the part of Tessa.

"Any time you're ready, Callie."

Meeting Caleb's gaze, Callie nodded, then began. It took a moment. Maybe two. After that, she lost herself, becoming Tessa. But her eyes never moved from Caleb's. The monologue was emotional. She was speaking to an empty room, but the words were to the man she loved. Callie delved deep into a well of emotion no twenty-year-old with her lack of personal experience should possess. Her mother called her an old soul. Her acting teacher called it instinct. Callie didn't understand why. She only knew that she always had the ability to push her true self aside so she could channel the character she wanted to portray.

Time slipped away. Straight through, Callie knew how long the monologue should last. Five minutes. She had timed it. However, when the last word left her mouth, an hour could have passed. Or a day. She had no concept of the minutes ticking away.

Blinking, Callie felt tired and exhilarated all at once. She had no doubt that she couldn't have done better. She had become Tessa. Now it was up to Caleb to decide if he agreed.

"Very nice." Caleb rose, holding out his hand.

That was it? Callie automatically put her hand in his, shaking it slowly. *Very nice*? She had poured her heart out—given all she could give—and all Caleb Landis had to say was *very nice*? Callie shifted her gaze toward T.K. What she saw wasn't much better. He looked a bit bemused, shrugging without a word.

"I can do it again." Callie wasn't sure how to change a reading she felt to her soul was near perfection. But if Caleb needed something different, she would try her damnedest to give it to him.

"No." Caleb moved to the door, opening it wide. "Thank you for coming in, Callie."

Confused beyond words, Callie shook T.K.'s hand before slowly leaving the office. Even at her worst auditions, she was given more feedback than Caleb's toneless response. Was she that bad? Had her performance been so bad it knocked the charm and warmth right out of him?

Callie was a big girl. She didn't expect everybody to gush over her. What she did expect was common courtesy. As she passed Caleb, his expression stoic, she wouldn't have been at all surprised if he gave her a firm kick in the ass. He had already booted her ego out the door, why not give her body the same treatment?

Stepping into the elevator, Callie slumped against the wall. The day had begun with so much hope and promise. So sure she had this, defeat was a bitter pill to swallow. Right now it was stuck in her throat, a big lump making it hard to breathe. In a day or two, she would pick herself up. Right now, Callie needed help dissolving the disappointment. Leaving the building, she knew exactly who to call.

Jack Daniels. He wasn't a friend she turned to very often, but when she did, he could be relied upon to make things better—at least for a night.

CHAPTER THREE

"WHAT THE HELL was that?" T.K. poured two cups of coffee from the outrageously expensive contraption in the corner of the office. Leaving them black, he handed one to Caleb. "Callie Flynn *is* Tessa. I had my doubts when you told me her age and experience. But come on. That reading gave me chills. Hell, there are chills on top of my chills."

"I agree." Not taking a drink, Caleb frowned into his cup.

"I understand not wanting to commit to anything until we talked it over, but you were cold, Caleb. *Very nice?* Screw that. Callie was beyond my wildest dreams. Tessa personified. I believed every word that came out of her mouth." T.K. rubbed his hands together, his smile gleeful. "I cannot wait to get her in front of a camera."

Caleb, his expression neutral, listened with half an ear as T.K. rhapsodized over Callie Flynn. Inside, he felt as if a semi had run him down—full speed ahead. Then for good measure, hit reverse, rolling back over his already mangled body. Except it wasn't a truck that took him out. It was a Callie Flynn. Not with the might of her five-foot-six-inch frame, but with her words. And those eyes. *Mother of God.* When she turned the power of her gaze on him, Caleb almost forgot how to breathe.

This had never happened to Caleb—not even close. He was a big man with a big sexual appetite. He took a woman to his bed when the urge dictated—which was often. Sometimes it lasted past one night. Sometimes it didn't. Either way, Caleb gave as good as he got. He was a man who found as much enjoyment in giving pleasure as receiving it.

However, it always ended, with never the slightest temptation to make things permanent. If the lady of the moment dropped the slightest hint that she was looking for more than some fun and games, Caleb dropped her. Like removing a Band-Aid. He made it as fast and painless as possible.

Caleb met beautiful, talented, interesting women all the time. What made Callie Flynn different? When she smiled, his heartbeat skittered slightly from its normal beat. When he inadvertently breathed in her fresh, spicy scent, he wanted to run his tongue along the curve of her neck—just to find out if she tasted half as good. He found those things disconcerting. But Caleb prided himself on his reputation as a professional. Putting aside his personal feelings—no matter how unexpectedly intense—wasn't a problem.

The meeting ran smoothly. Caleb found Callie to be bright and quick-witted. She had an easy smile that he knew from watching her movies, translated beautifully onto film as did her winning personality. What she had went far below the surface. With the proper technique, faking emotions was not difficult for an actor. Meeting Callie in person, he was certain what she put into her characters was genuine.

Caleb looked forward to hearing her read the part of Tessa. How was he supposed to know her eyes would mesmerize? That the way she spoke the words he knew so well would be a revelation. His reaction to Callie Flynn—the actress *and* the woman—was something Caleb couldn't have anticipated.

When Callie finished the monologue, he didn't know how to respond. She looked so pleased. So hopeful. And all he could say was *very nice*. Talk about major understatements. Unfortunately, at that moment, it was all he could manage. His emotions were in turmoil. If he had let himself say more, who knew what might have poured from his mouth. Damn certain it would have embarrassed both of them.

"She was spectacular."

"Yes!" T.K. shouted. "Finally. Why didn't you say that before?"

Caleb sipped his coffee, his eyes narrowed. There was no way in hell he would tell T.K. what had happened. The man was one of his closest friends, but how could he explain something when *he* didn't understand it? Physical attraction was one thing. Easy. Simple. This was more. Caleb had moved into unknown territory. Until he had his bearings, nobody could know.

"We'll let her know." Casually, Caleb tossed the script onto his desk. "Callie Flynn is our Tessa."

"Damn straight." Taking Caleb's words at face value, T.K. let the rest slide. "We can start filming by the end of the month. I know the budget is tight."

"That's putting it mildly," Caleb laughed, relieved at the change of subject. "I'm counting on you to bring the shoot in on time."

"On time?" T.K. looked offended. "I have a reputation to maintain. If this movie doesn't wrap ahead of schedule, I will eat my lucky fedora."

That was saying something. T.K. wore the same hat on set since his directorial debut. It had seen better days—to say the least. However, unless the Smithsonian came calling, retirement was not an option.

"I'll keep reminding you of that."

Caleb wasn't worried. T.K. Paulson's movies never ran over budget. Like death and taxes, it was guaranteed.

With a sigh, T.K. rubbed the back of his neck. "I can tell you, my friend, I was starting to think Tessa didn't exist. I can't believe how lucky we are that you saw her in that restaurant."

Had it been luck? Or fate? Caleb had never been one to believe in such things. *He* made things happen. *He* controlled his life. Still, when Callie started the monologue—looking into his eyes—there had been a feeling of inevitability.

Caleb shook off his fanciful thoughts. He had a movie to produce and other projects in the early stages. He didn't have time to think about chance meetings or destiny. As far as he was concerned, there was no such thing. However, just for his peace of mind, he planned on staying far away from the *Meant to Be* set and far, far away from Callie Flynn.

"YOU HAVE A meeting at ten. Lunch with Dustin Hoffman at twelve-thirty. The rough-cut of *Priceless Ending* will be set up in the screening room this afternoon." Nadine handed Caleb the morning mail. "And what is going on? You look like crap."

"You would bash me over the head with this stack of letters if I said that to you." Caleb knew he looked like a man who worked too many hours and suffered too many sleepless nights. The last thing he wanted was his assistant shoving the obvious in his face.

"True." Nadine sat opposite him. She never left her desk without a pad and pen in her hand, always ready to jot down notes or pertinent information. She set the items on Caleb's desk, signaling that this was personal, not business. "After I hit you, I would realize your comment was said with friendly concern."

"Duly noted." Blindly taking the first letter from the pile, Caleb hoped to put an end to the discussion. He should have known better.

"Are you in financial trouble?"

"What?" Caleb shook his head with a small smile. "Don't worry. I can meet payroll for a few more months."

"You know if you were in financial trouble I would stay without pay until you got back on your feet." Nadine's tone and expression told Caleb that she didn't find any humor in the subject. "If you don't want to talk about what's bothering you, say so. But do not question my loyalty."

"I'm sorry." With a deep sigh, Caleb ran a hand over his face. "I couldn't function without you, Nadine. You're my right arm and my friend."

"That's all I needed to hear." The fierce light in Nadine's eyes softened. "As your friend, I want you to know you can always talk to me. Even if you don't want advice, sometimes it helps to verbalize a problem."

Caleb hesitated. Trust wasn't the issue. Anything he told Nadine was more secure than Fort Knox. Resting his arms on his desk, he decided he had to do something. The chances of driving himself crazy inched closer and closer with each passing day.

"It's a woman." When Nadine's eyes widened, her mouth opening and closing without comment, Caleb threw up his hands. "What?"

"It's just…" Nadine seemed to struggle for the right words—a rarity for his assistant. "Women fall at your feet. Literally. Remember the reporter? She took one look at you and went flying."

"She tripped over a camera cable."

"Because you smiled at her. Face it, boss, women love you. They never turn you down." Nadine whistled. "Is that it? Has the unimaginable happened? Caleb Landis, the mighty Sex God, has been rejected?"

Caleb knew that Nadine was only half teasing. He had a well-earned reputation. When he wanted a woman, she usually returned the interest. Honestly, he couldn't remember the last time he was romantically shot down. He was sure it must have happened. Once or twice. Years ago.

"I haven't asked her."

"Why not? Oh, crap. Is she married? Engaged? A nun?"

"A nun?" Where the hell did Nadine come up with these things?

"I just read *The Thornbirds*. The character was a priest instead of a nun. And he gave into his passions. Good book. I hear it's going to be made into a TV mini-series." Realizing she veered far from the original topic, Nadine pulled herself back. "You don't have the hots for a bride of Christ?"

"When you put it like that it sounds even worse. And no. To all your questions."

"Then what's the problem?"

"She's the lead in my latest movie."

"Callie Flynn. Isn't she a little young?"

Age hadn't entered Caleb's mind. Yet it was the first thing out of Nadine's mouth. Callie came across as such a mature woman. He considered himself to be young—in the prime of his life. To him, it was a non-issue.

"I'm seven years older than she is. That hardly makes me a dirty old man."

"Fine," Nadine nodded. "What is the problem? The movie will wrap by mid-December. Two months is not a big deal." Nadine waited for Caleb to agree. When he didn't, her eyebrows rose. "Or is it?"

"I don't know."

That wasn't an easy admission. Caleb had always been able to prioritize—weed out the unimportant to concentrate on what was vital at that moment. His career came first. Always. Callie Flynn was like a song Caleb couldn't stop humming. At the oddest times, she snuck past his defenses. Check that. She was close to toppling them altogether. And it scared the hell out of him.

"I can't get Callie Flynn out of my head.

"There is a simple solution."

Desperate, Caleb leaned forward, anxious for any port in the storm.

"Well?" he demanded when Nadine shook her head.

"Men. Why does that dangling piece of flesh between your legs dictate so much of your lives?"

Caleb wanted to take issue with Nadine's statement. Unfortunately, it was too close to the truth for comfort. All he had in the way of a comeback was a mumbled, "Hormones?"

As if he hadn't spoken, Nadine tsked. "Don't get me wrong. I'm a big fan of the male species. I approve of the physical differences between men and women. The deep timbre of your voices. How you are hard where we are soft. For somebody who loves the act of kissing—for me—men are imperative. That said…"

"Yes?" Caleb asked with more than a little trepidation. Something told him he was not going to like Nadine's next words. But like a book he wasn't particularly enjoying, with only a chapter left, he had to find out how it ended.

"When it comes to women, you haven't a clue."

"That's it?" Caleb had hung on Nadine's every word, waiting for pearls of wisdom. Instead, she told him what he had figured out soon after he hit puberty.

"There's more. Take sex out of the equation."

Caleb simply crossed his arms, his expression blank.

"Hear me out," Nadine chuckled. "Why not exchange sex for romance? Send Callie flowers. Go for a long walk while holding hands. Ask about her life. About her family. About her childhood. Have you ever simply spent time with a woman when you knew that getting her into bed was not an option?"

Not since he was sixteen—the year he had sex for the first time. These days, he didn't have the time—or the inclination. Until now. Mulling over Nadine's suggestion, Caleb found the idea more and more appealing. Maybe he *was* getting old. Or maybe the difference maker was Callie Flynn.

"May I ask you a question?"

Nadine's expression turned leery. "I guess it's only fair, considering."

"Why do you keep turning down T.K.? If you asked, I know he would be happy to romance you before hopping into bed."

"Oh, Caleb," Nadine sighed. "You really *don't* understand, do you?"

"I want to."

"I suppose that's something." Picking up her pad and pen, Nadine rose. "Most women want to be romanced. However, we shouldn't have to ask for it."

After Nadine had left, Caleb sat for a long time, mulling over what she had told him. Her points were valid. Women wanted romance. Even deserved it. For their sakes, he hoped they found a man who wanted to give it to them. That man was not him.

Caleb had no regrets. He had always been courteous to his date's needs. Kind. Charming. During the few hours they were together—through dinner and after-meal activities—his attention never wavered. But romance? Long walks? Intense talks? Sorry, it wasn't who he was.

Then Caleb thought of Callie. Perhaps his willingness to explore a different path was less about him and more about her. His feelings were a jumbled mess. Did he want to take the time to figure them out? Did he want to get to know Callie with no guarantee of any intimacy beyond holding her hand?

· It didn't take long for Caleb to figure out the answer. No matter what. No matter how it ended. Right now, he wanted to be with Callie. It was as simple—and complicated—as that.

That decided, Caleb felt a weight lift from his chest. Something told him that tonight sleep would not be a problem. With a bemused smile, he hit the intercom button.

"Yes?" Nadine answered.

Normally, when Caleb needed a personal errand, he asked Nadine to take care of it. But this was different. This was for Callie.

"I need to order some flowers. Get me the name of a florist within walking distance."

CHAPTER FOUR

THE CARNATIONS ARRIVED at Callie's trailer her first morning on set. She was still marveling at the unexpected luxury of having her own space when she heard a knock at the door. Expecting somebody from the movie crew, she was surprised to find a delivery man holding a crystal vase wrapped with a white satin bow and four dozen cheery yellow flowers.

"Callie Flynn?" the young man asked, checking his clipboard. When he looked up into her bright gray eyes, his smile widened.

"Are those for me?"

The second the words were out of her mouth Callie knew it was a silly question. The man wore a dark blue uniform emblazoned with a logo from *Bismarck Florists.* He knew her name. He stood outside of *her* trailer. Of course, the flowers were for her. Who else?

"Would you like me to bring them in for you?"

"I think I can handle it."

Did the delivery man honestly think she would invite him into her trailer? And do what, Callie wondered. Happily, she would never have to find out. Taking the vase from his reluctant hands, she backed away. Normally, she would have given him a tip. It was without an ounce of guilt that she quickly shut the door. Callie figured anybody who leered like that, didn't deserve a penny of her hard-earned money.

Callie had always scoffed at the thought of cut flowers. While roses were nice, they were nothing to her but a pretty cliché. Before their senior prom, her friends hinted heavily for gardenias or orchids as a corsage. Callie thought it a lot of fuss, bother, and expense for something that would wither in a day or two.

As she breathed in the carnations' spicy aroma, Callie wondered if she needed to rethink her stance. The thought that somebody had gone out of their way to order the blooms in her honor sent a burst of pleasure through her body. Anxious to find out who she needed to thank, Callie reached for the attached card as another knock sounded at her door.

"Mr. Landis." Speaking of bursts of pleasure. "Good morning."

"It's Caleb. Remember, Callie."

"Of course. You'll have to forgive me. First day jitters." And the fact that her boss—her uncomfortably sexy boss—had dropped by unexpectedly.

"It's kind of like the first day at a new school."

Callie laughed. "That's exactly what I was thinking." Suddenly, she realized where they were. "I'm sorry for making you stand there. Would you like to come in?"

"Another time." Caleb looked at his watch. "I think you're due at the hair and makeup trailer. May I walk with you?"

For a second, the way Caleb phrased the question threw Callie. *May I walk with you?* It felt personal—almost intimate. As if he were speaking to her as a man, not a producer. *Whoa.* Callie mentally gave herself a slap. *Do not go down that road, young lady.* Caleb Landis paid her salary. He called the shots. As attractive as she found him, he was off limits.

"Let me grab my bag."

Popping inside, Callie slung the carry-all over her shoulder. The contents revolved around the situation, but always contained certain things she couldn't do without. What she called her movie set essentials. A book for the inevitable downtime. A pack of chewing gum. *Chap Stick* to keep her lips moist. A comb. And a comfortable pair of shoes. Having these things nearby saved somebody the job of running back to her trailer between shots.

Deciding she had everything she needed, Callie was just about to join Caleb when out of the corner of her eye she caught sight of the flowers. And the attached card. Not wanting to wait all morning to find out who sent the carnations, she grabbed the tiny envelope before exiting the trailer.

"That bag is almost bigger than you." Caleb fell in step with Callie as she took the path to her right.

Callie patted the worn leather satchel. "I've had this baby since high school. Before that, my father carried it through Southeast Asia. He was a war correspondent in Vietnam."

"You were just a kid. It must have been tough on you and your mother to have him gone."

Callie nodded. "I was ten years old. Not that young. Until then, Dad had stuck close to home. He worked for the local CBS affiliate. The chance to report on the biggest news story of the day was a huge promotion. He told my mother it was up to her. He knew it wasn't fair to leave her alone with three children.

They didn't talk about the danger. Partly for the sake of my sisters and me. But much later, Mom told me that if she had let herself dwell on what might happen, she never would have survived the two years he was gone."

Caleb sent Callie a probing look. "I spent those years in college. Protesting the war."

"My family did the same. Dad did his bit on national television. Mom carried the banner at home." Feeling a connection to him, Callie placed her hand on Caleb's arm as if it were something she did all the time. "I had friends who lost loved ones. Brothers. Uncles. Fathers. We were lucky. Dad came home."

Caleb's hand covered hers. "It was impossible to live through that time and not lose somebody you knew. I'm glad your Dad survived."

They walked the rest of the way in silence. In a few short minutes, they had found common ground. Callie felt a bond with Caleb. Unexpected. Tentative. Yet it felt surprisingly solid.

"I'll leave you here." Caleb held Callie's hand for several heartbeats, his smile warm and friendly.

"Goodbye."

With a wave, Callie entered the trailer.

"You must be our leading lady." A tall, slender man with skin the color of rich chocolate stood behind a beautician's chair. He patted the shiny red vinyl. "Hop on, Callie Flynn. My name is Lange."

Callie settled into the seat. She knew the routine. She always enjoyed this time before work began. Having her hair and makeup done by a professional was still a novelty. She felt pampered. Special. It didn't matter that he would perform the same service for the rest of the cast. Here and now, she was the center of attention. She would be a fool not to enjoy it.

"Lange? Is that your first or last name?"

"Both. Like Cher. Or Elvis." Lange said, his tone matter-of-fact. He turned Callie to face the mirror that hung above a counter crowded with every kind of beauty product imaginable. Staring long and hard at her image, he let out a heartfelt sigh. "You are not what I was expecting."

"Okay." Callie drew out the word.

"Now don't get your panties in a twist. I didn't mean that as an insult. Just the opposite." Lange picked up several clips, pulling Callie's hair away from her face. "They told me to make you beautiful. In my head, that meant you had talent, but were lacking in the beauty department. It would be up to me to give you pizzazz." He pushed several pots of foundation out of the way before dipping a sponge into the one of his choosing and dabbing it onto Callie's face. "Baby, you are stunning. How am I supposed to improve on perfection?"

Callie laughed. She liked Lange and had the feeling they would be fast friends. As long as she took his propensity for outrageous exaggerations with a massive grain of salt.

After an hour, Callie's hair and makeup were perfect—according to Lange. Her next visit was to wardrobe. Nothing fancy. A summery dress, sandals, and a lightweight shawl completed her ensemble. The character of Tessa didn't have a lot of money. Her clothes were neat, clean, and simple. Luckily, her personality was infinitely more complicated.

To an outsider, the set looked like utter chaos. People ran from point to point, shouting to be heard over the sound of other people who were running and shouting. To Callie, it felt like home. She stood on the sidelines, taking it all in.

"Callie," T.K. called out, motioning her over. He was dressed in a pair of old jeans, sneakers, a faded t-shirt. And of course, the famous fedora. "Are you ready to make a masterpiece?"

It seemed Callie had waited her entire life for somebody to ask her that. Knowing it was bit cheesy, she couldn't resist. With a wink, she said her line with perfect timing.

"I was born ready."

"CUT AND PRINT. Let's call it a day. Callie? Hold up."

Caleb watched from his place behind an unused piece of equipment as T.K. jogged over to Callie. He placed an arm around her shoulders, dipping his head. It was impossible to hear what he said, but it must have been good. Callie threw back her head, her laughter making him smile. And—to his consternation—drawing appreciative looks from several crew members.

Jealousy. Though not an emotion Caleb knew from personal experience, he had no problem recognizing it. Callie Flynn brought out all kinds of new feelings. Caleb was through fighting, but he had no idea what he wanted from Callie. Their brief conversation that morning made it clear they could be friends. The heat that shot through his body from the mere touch of her hand proved that he wanted her as his lover. And then? Caleb couldn't say. Not yet.

32

Deciding he had made a good start with Callie, Caleb was about to leave when Abe Pickens greeted him with a slap on the back. The man had been in Hollywood since the early forties. He had worked with all the greats from Bogart to Brando. Over the years, his job description had changed, working his way up from script supervisor to assistant director. Never aspiring to the top job, Abe made a good living doing what he loved. He was happy to leave the headaches of being in charge to somebody else.

"How's it going, kid?"

Abe called everybody kid. Not because he was lousy with names—the man had a computer for a brain. It was simply his way.

"I love the first day of a shoot." Standing shoulder to shoulder with the Hollywood veteran, Caleb surveyed the set. "The possibilities are endless. Even if you know the script is crap, at least for one day, this one might be an Oscar contender."

"Hope springs eternal." Abe crossed his arms over his barrel of a chest, the muscles of his arms bulging. Once a stuntman, he was in better shape than most men half his age. "Not that you have to worry about this one. It's a winner."

"I think so," Caleb agreed. Still, it was nice to hear it from a person he respected.

"And speaking of winners." Abe nodded toward Callie as she and T.K. continued their conversation. "There is something special about that young lady."

That wasn't news to Caleb. Callie had drawn him in from the moment he saw her. With each meeting, she seemed to wrap him in an invisible bond that was beyond his power to break. It was a mystery. Perhaps Abe had the answer.

"*Why* is Callie Flynn special?"

Abe laughed. Hard. Wiping the moisture from his eyes, the older man shook his head. "You've been around this business long enough to know there is no one answer to that question."

Maybe not, but Caleb needed something. Anything to help him explain why he couldn't get this particular woman out of his head.

"Humor me."

As if he could sense Caleb's desperation, Abe sent him a half smile.

"Callie is beautiful."

That was it? "The world is filled with beautiful women," Caleb grumbled.

"Her talent is obvious."

"Again, talent isn't that unusual."

"If you plan on interrupting me every five seconds, this is going to take all night."

Caleb didn't understand the purpose of stating the obvious. That said, he had asked. Abe had the prerogative to answer in his own time and his own way—no matter how frustrating.

"I apologize." Caleb inclined his head. "Please. Continue."

"Beauty and talent. As you said, they are a dime a dozen. If the actress has luck on her side, she can have a big career. Then there are the Callie Flynns of the world. She's part of a rare breed. She has that undefinable something that comes along once or twice in a generation. You saw it immediately. It has nothing to do with luck. There's no formula. You can't manufacture what she has. Quite simply, the young woman is a star. Now. Tomorrow. Thirty years from now. Trust me. You can write it in stone."

In other words, Caleb was screwed. Or blessed. It depended on how he chose to look at things. Callie—and everything she represented for him—was inevitable? Was that what Abe was telling him?

"My wife would call it destiny." Abe seemed to find the idea amusing.

"You don't believe in such a thing?" Caleb never had. Now, he wasn't as certain.

"I like to keep an open mind." Abe scratched his head, messing up the thick dark mop that was liberally salted with gray. "It's pretty much what I was saying. You could fire Callie Flynn tomorrow. She would land on her feet. Hell, she would thrive. Look at her. Do you have any doubts?"

Caleb didn't have to look. He hadn't taken his eyes off Callie. As for doubts? Nope. Not even a sliver. In her element, she glowed.

"Callie is a star."

"Exactly." Shifting his gaze to Caleb, Abe shot him a knowing look. "Is Callie Flynn the one?"

Caleb could have huffed and puffed and denied. Instead, he let out a sigh.

"I've known her for less than a month. Spoken to her a handful of times."

"Love at first sight isn't a myth, kid. It happened to me."

"Daphne?"

Nodding, Abe smiled. His memories were his own, but the love he felt for his wife was written on his face for the world to see. "My lady and I will celebrate fifty-two years in January."

It wasn't an inconceivable amount of time. Caleb's parents were approaching their thirtieth anniversary. However, for a marriage to last that long, there had to be a beginning. A day one. A wedding. It was the kind of commitment he always planned on making—someday.

"Kid, you've turned white as a ghost." Giving Caleb's arm a shake, Abe chuckled. "Calm down. You have time to figure it out."

Time. Caleb had time. Saying it to himself over and over had a calming effect. "Any advice?"

"Slow down. Get to know the lady. But don't take too long. Callie Flynn is a keeper. If you don't make your move soon, you can bet another man will. Got to go," Abe waved at a beckoning crew member. "Take it easy, kid."

Absently, Caleb rubbed the side of his neck. Nothing Abe had told him was a revelation. Callie was special. She had a blindingly bright career ahead of her. On a personal level, he would be a fool to think there was an open field where she was concerned. Men liked to watch Callie. Even when doing their jobs, the crew had kept one eye on her. She drew attention without the least bit of effort.

Let them look, Caleb thought, his blues eyes darkening, his chin firm with determination. Soon, everybody would fall in love with Callie Flynn. The thought of sharing the actress with the world, doing everything in his power to boost her career into the stratosphere.

The private Callie was a different matter. He wanted her. She held a chunk of his heart in those lovely hands of hers. Damned if he would be in this quagmire of emotion alone.

A slow smile spread across Caleb's face. Feeling a sense of calm, he took his keys from his pocket, feeling on solid ground for the first time in weeks.

Watch out, Callie Flynn. Caleb Landis is out to win your heart. And when he puts his mind to something, he never fails.

CHAPTER FIVE

THE CLOCK RADIO read ten minutes until five. Callie's alarm was set to ring at the top of the hour and those few minutes until the rock station began to blare were precious. She had a long, intense day ahead of her. She needed every bit of rest she could get.

Since she was wide awake and trying to get back to sleep would be pointless, Callie took the card from under her pillow before pulling the covers under her chin. She didn't need to turn on a light to know what was written on the piece of paper. By now she had it memorized.

Good luck on your first day. Caleb.

It was hardly dripping with suppressed emotion and romance. Then why did the handwritten words make Callie's heart pound and her stomach flutter with the wings of a thousand butterflies? Again and again, she chided herself for reading more into a simple gesture of flowers, and a generic message that Caleb probably sent to every actress on the first day of shooting.

The half snort, half snore from the other bed broke into Callie's musings. Reaching over, she turned off the alarm two minutes before it was due to go off. Just because she had to be up before dawn didn't mean her roommate's sleep should be interrupted.

Slipping from the bed, her feet hit the ratty carpet. She knew the worn shag was clean because the first thing she did before moving in was rent a bulky carpet cleaner from the neighborhood supermarket. That, and scrub every inch of the bathroom she shared with three less than fastidious women. Callie shuddered when she thought of the things she found growing in the shower or the shocking state of the toilet.

Callie's apartment mates were slobs—plain and simple. However, they were pleased when she cleaned the place from top to bottom. Realizing that she was in a position to save herself a few bucks, she brokered a deal. They paid part of her rent. In return, she kept the place from looking like a moldy science experiment gone horribly wrong.

There was one good thing about rising early. Instead of hoping for enough hot water after three previous showers, Callie enjoyed the steamy water to her heart's content. Regretfully, this morning she barely had time for more than a quick in and out. She had to be on the set, hair and makeup done, by seven o'clock.

Callie towel dried her hair, quickly running a comb through the tangles. Quickly, she rubbed lotion over her skin—top to bottom—then threw on a pair of jeans, a comfortable sweater, and a dab of lip balm. Having a car pick her up each morning and drive her home at night was a luxury Callie could happily become accustomed to. However, she refused to act the diva by keeping the driver waiting. Checking the time, Callie grabbed her satchel. Five minutes to spare. Pleased, her sneakered feet took the stairs at a leisurely jog. The street outside the apartment building was lined with parked cars. A cursory inspection told her that her ride was yet to arrive. Knowing she wouldn't have long to wait, Callie took a seat on the stoop, rummaging through her bag for something to snack on. Cookies weren't exactly the breakfast of champions, but they would do in a pinch.

Victory! Callie broke open the package. Taking a bite of sweet, chocolate chip goodness, she closed her eyes, leaning back to rest her elbows on the concrete steps. A cookie, a car that delivered her onto the set of her dream job, and a few moments of quiet. Could life get any better? In the next instant, her question was answered with a great big hell yes.

"Need a ride?"

In case she was dreaming, Callie kept her eyes closed.

"Caleb?"

"Why don't you put those cookies away and let me buy you a proper breakfast?"

Callie scrunched her face, opening her eyelids enough for a tiny peek. Definitely not a dream. Though Caleb Landis was the definition of dreamy. She didn't know why he was standing less than three feet away, dressed in a suit that probably cost more than she paid in rent for a year, but at the moment she didn't care. He was so pretty, she opened her eyes all the way and enjoyed the view.

"Is this some kind of test?" Callie teased, her lips twitching. Caleb Landis had a reputation as a bottom-line producer. She doubted he really wanted her to play hooky. "I have a job. On your movie. Remember?"

"The shoot has been delayed until this afternoon. The water pipes burst at the high school where you were scheduled to film."

When it looked like Caleb was about to sit next to her, Callie held out her hand.

"Wait." She opened her satchel, pulling out an oversized handkerchief. Carefully, she laid it down. "These steps are chipped and gritty. It would be a shame to ruin that beautiful suit."

"Callie." Shaking his head, Caleb chuckled. Picking up the handkerchief, he shook it out before tucking it back into her bag. "It wouldn't be gentlemanly. Not when you don't have one."

"Seriously?" When he nodded, Callie laughed. "I'm wearing jeans that have seen better days. You're wearing?" She touched the lapel of his jacket, running the material between her fingers. "Oh, my Lord, that is soft. Wool gabardine?"

"Impressive. The shirt and tie are silk. But feel free to find out for yourself."

Looking up, Callie found her face inches from Caleb's. The clever quip on the tip of her tongue dissolved like the snowflakes she used to chase as a girl. *Such blue eyes*, she thought, licking her lips.

It was one of those moments life often threw at the unsuspecting. A turning point. Callie could lean in, making it clear she wanted Caleb's kiss. Or she could play it smart and ease away. No fuss. No muss. She was a hairsbreadth from throwing caution to the wind when Caleb moved first. To her surprise, *he* was the sensible one, distancing himself before their lips could touch.

"Breakfast?" Caleb held out his hand.

Callie let Caleb pull her to her feet. Keeping hold of her hand, he picked up her satchel, slinging it over his shoulder.

"One question," Callie asked as they crossed the street.

"Ask as many as you want."

"One will do—to start. Do you always send flowers to your leading ladies?"

"You're the first." Caleb stopped beside a dark blue Jaguar.

"Nice car." Callie ran her hand over the sleek line of the hood.

"Want to drive?"

"Yes." She laughed when Caleb held out the keys. "Another time."

Sliding into the passenger seat, Callie marveled at the ultra-soft leather seats. Breathing, she sighed. New car. There was nothing like that smell. Not surprisingly, the more expensive the vehicle, the more potent the smell.

"Where would you like to go?" Caleb started the car, the engine purring like a contented cat—the large, African variety.

"Beats me. I'm dressed for the corner diner. You look like you stepped off the cover of *GQ*. We don't exactly match."

"Really?" Caleb's blue gaze met Callie's, his lips curving into a warm smile. "I think we go together perfectly."

How was I supposed to take that? Callie sat back as he drove from the parking spot, her mind swirling with the possibilities. Caleb had told her she could ask as many questions as she wanted. She went with the first one that popped into her head.

"Is this a date?"

"Yes."

"Oh." Callie hadn't expected such a quick answer. Or such a brief one. "I don't know how I feel about that. You *are* my boss."

"Would you feel better if I told you this *isn't* a date?"

"You mean lie?" Caleb nodded. "Do you meet women who want that?"

"You'd be surprised."

"Not really." Callie wasn't jaded. However, she had seen enough since leaving Iowa to understand that a lot of people did not consider honesty to be the best policy. "I want you to tell me the truth, Caleb. About my acting. About our friendship. About everything."

"That goes both ways, Callie." Showing an impressive amount of expertise, Caleb parallel parked in front of *Instant Gratification*. Callie had heard of the restaurant but never been. "I hope we get to a point where we can trust each other. Friends is a good place to start."

"I'd like that."

Callie had a handful of friends in Los Angeles—none of them particularly close. Maneuvering the ins and outs of Hollywood could be exhausting. Callie spent the first three months alternating between anger and despair. More than once, she would stand in the shower, rinsing herself clean while crying out her frustrations and homesickness. That had passed as she grew accustomed to the big city and developed a thicker skin.

Callie took Caleb's hand as he helped her from the car. She missed having somebody to confide in. A true friend. It was hard to tell if Caleb would turn out to be that person. She hoped so.

If nothing else, he was damn easy on the eyes, Callie chuckled to herself. Which brought her back to a problem that she had mentioned but hadn't been addressed.

"You're my boss. People will talk."

"People always talk." Caleb opened the door to the restaurant, guiding Callie inside.

They had arrived just ahead of the morning rush, so they didn't have to wait. The hostess led them to a table by the window, leaving them with menus and a promise to return with two coffees.

"I got this job on my merits, right?"

Caleb looked into Callie's eyes, his blue gaze devoid of the usual teasing glint. "You were hired because I know you're the only actress capable of playing Tessa."

The words Callie needed to hear. She didn't care what anybody thought. Let them speculate about how and why she was hired. From the first time an actress recited the spoken word in front of an audience, she had to deal with whispers and innuendo. She was often labeled a whore with nothing—beyond the fact that she painted her face and dared to grasp a bit of independence—to back up the claim.

Callie had it easier than her trailblazing counterparts. Society no longer frowned on her choice of profession. Just the opposite. An actress was revered. Worshipped. *If* she could achieve success. To do that, she had to avoid the pitfalls—ones that lurked behind the shady predators who claimed they could make her a star.

"For two years, I have bobbed and weaved my way through this town with the kind of moves an NFL running back would envy." Callie took a sip of coffee, sending a smile of thanks to their waitress. "Pancakes, please. A tall stack."

"I'll have the Denver omelet." Caleb handed back the menus.

When they were alone, Callie continued. "Do you know what I learned?"

"That men are pigs?" A half smile curved Caleb's lips.

"I discovered that the first time Tony Wilcox looked down my shirt in the seventh grade," Callie said with a shake of her head. Her eyes were the color of tempered steel. "It doesn't matter that I didn't sleep with you to get this part. The gossipmongers will believe what they believe. Let them. As long as *I* know the truth, I will sleep like a baby."

"I'm impressed." Genuine admiration shined in Caleb's gaze. "I know women, *and* men, who have worked in this business for decades and never reach your level of self-awareness." His blue eyes narrowed. "How old are you again?"

Callie's laugh was bright and genuine. She liked this man. *Liked* him. It had been a long time since she could say that about a member of the opposite sex.

"This friendship thing."

Caleb looked at her over the rim of his cup. "Yes?"

"Do you want more?"

"Define more."

Callie's eyes narrowed. She saw Caleb's lips twitch. He knew very well what she meant. It seemed he was going to make her say it.

"Do you want to have sex?"

"In general?" Caleb nodded somberly, yet a definite twinkle in his eyes. "I'm a big fan. I would say it ranks in my top five favorite activities."

Callie couldn't help herself. She had to ask.

"What are the other four?"

Caleb shook his head. "That's part of the friendship process. You'll find out—eventually."

Eventually. That made it sound like Caleb wanted them to spend a lot more time together. Callie approved wholeheartedly.

"As for sex with you?"

Her cup halfway to her mouth, Callie paused.

"Go on," she urged. "What about sex with me?"

Reaching across the table, Caleb laced his fingers with hers, his gaze falling to her parted lips.

"On that list of favorite activities? Number one. With a bullet."

CHAPTER SIX

THE SHOOTING SCHEDULE sailed along without any more delays. Callie found the work invigorating. For the first time in her career, she had the chance to stretch her acting chops to the breaking point. Just when she thought she had nothing left, T.K. demanded more. Somehow—somewhere deep inside—Callie found reserves she never guessed existed.

It was exhilarating. Terrifying. Exhausting. In other words, making *Meant to Be* was the greatest experience of Callie's life. This was what she had dreamed about in her tiny childhood bedroom. In her mind, she acted out great lines, written by brilliant authors. Yes, she wanted to be a star. But it wouldn't mean anything if the end product wasn't something she was proud of. This script. This movie. It was going to be a classic. Callie was certain all the way down to her bones.

The one fly in her ointment was Preston Marsh. Her leading man was talented. He was known for playing the type of character female audiences swooned over. It made him perfect for the part of Felix—the love of Tessa's life. The man she would sacrifice everything to keep safe.

In real life, Callie didn't find Preston worth the time it would take her to cross the street. Unfortunately, his ego made him deaf to her rebuffs. If anything, the more she said no, the harder he pushed. One thing kept her from pushing back. The movie. It came first. She could put up with Preston. On her annoyance meter, he was a gnat. Hard to get rid of but basically harmless.

"This is the last big romantic moment between you and Preston." T.K. pulled Callie aside, his words for her ears only. "After this, your scenes range from cold to antagonistic."

"Hallelujah."

"You promised to tell me if Preston wasn't behaving himself. Has something changed?"

T.K. had witnessed Preston attempting to pat Callie on the ass. Before he could ream Preston out, Callie handled the situation. She grabbed her leading man by the thumb, twisting until he landed on his knees, pleading for her to turn him loose. T.K. had added a graphic warning. The incident had happened in earshot of the cast and crew. Since then, Preston had kept his hands to himself. For the most part.

"I would tell you if anything happened that I couldn't handle." When Callie saw that T.K. wasn't convinced, she playfully punched him in the arm. "Relax. Like you said, after today, I won't have to play nice—on or off camera."

"I should have told Caleb—"

"You agreed, T.K. For the good of the movie." Callie was appalled at the idea. "Besides, it's none of Caleb's business."

"Wrong. First, he's producing this film. Everything that impacts the final product is Caleb's business." T.K. held up his hand, lowering a finger every time he ticked off one of his points. "Second..."

"Yes?" Callie waited, crossing her arms, her gaze steady. She knew what T.K. was thinking. Would he go there?

"He has a personal interest in you."

"We are tentatively dating." Callie smiled, pleased with her turn of phrase. "It doesn't make Caleb my keeper. The same would be true of any man in my life. I can take care of myself. In fact, I insist on it."

T.K. threw his hands up in the air. "Why are women so touchy?"

"Why are men so clueless?"

"I don't know." T.K. shifted his attention over Callie's shoulder. "Why don't we ask Caleb?"

"Ask me what?"

Callie suppressed her groan, but the warning look she sent T.K. spoke volumes. Apparently, something she said had gotten through to him. The subject of Preston Marsh had been shelved. Hopefully for good.

"What do you think of the dress Callie's wearing?"

Playing along, Callie twirled, the blue rayon skirt teasingly brushing her legs.

"Great?" Caleb looked perplexed. He had approved wardrobe long ago. "Is there a problem?"

"I wondered if a brighter color would be better." Callie wasn't lying. It was something she thought the first time she saw the dress. It felt a bit somber for such a happy moment. "We're shooting the big reunion scene. Red is obvious. But maybe yellow? Or at least a cheerier blue?"

Callie had to give Caleb points for seeming to seriously consider his answer. "Blue suits you. Maybe a different shade would be better. What do you think, T.K.?"

"Work it out with wardrobe, Callie." Shaking his head, T.K. gave Callie a slight tip of his head as if acknowledging how quickly she thought on her feet. "Did you need me for something?"

"Just checking in," Caleb said with a casual shrug.

"Funny. I don't recall you doing that on any other film."

"Are you complaining?" Caleb gave T.K. a long, pointed look. "Has my presence disrupted your set?"

"I didn't say that," T.K. gritted out through clenched teeth. Muttering to himself, he strode away. "I swear there is something in the water."

"Do you want to tell me what that was about?"

Callie should have known he hadn't fallen for *the color of my dress* excuse.

"Will you take my word for it when I tell you it isn't important and let it drop?"

"That depends." Caleb searched Callie's face. "Could I make the situation better?"

"Maybe." Callie sighed. "Probably. I'm asking you to let me take care of it in my own way. I have so far."

"This is an ongoing problem? And it has to do with the movie? Callie—"

Callie had only known Caleb for a short time, but she recognized that he was revving up for a potential explosion. "I'm fine and so is your movie. You're happy with the dailies?"

Caleb's blue eyes narrowed as if he sensed a trick. "You know I am."

"Then why look for trouble when none exists?"

"Because I can tell you're keeping something from me." Caleb reached for her hand, thinking better of it at the last second, holding his fist firmly at his side. "I will let it slide. This time."

Caleb's frustration was palpable. He was used to getting his way in all things. In business *and* personally. Though this was their first clash on the set, he had found out quickly that she wasn't a pushover on the dating front. They were playing by her rules—a first for Caleb Landis.

Callie enjoyed taking things slow—getting to know Caleb little by little. They would share a sandwich in her trailer or walk around the set, talking the entire time. Their conversations weren't structured. She would ask about his childhood and end up learning how he had spent one summer working on a road crew in Sicily. Caleb had traveled to places Callie had never heard of. Villages that didn't warrant even the tiniest dot on a map. His descriptions were colorful. As were his stories. Though he made the places come to life, she longed to see the dirt roads and ancient ruins in person—with him at her side.

Realizing what she was doing, Callie brought her thoughts to a screeching halt. A shot of fear raced up her spine. Too fast. Too soon. She and Caleb were having fun. They hadn't even kissed—though the thought had crossed her mind more than once. This was perfect. Fun was all she wanted. She didn't have room in her life for anything more.

Keep it light. Keep it simple. For Callie, they were words to live by.

"Would you like to get something to eat?" Caleb looked at his watch, unaware of Callie's jumbled musings. "I have an hour before I need to be back to the office."

"I have to take care of my dress." Callie smiled, but it didn't reach her eyes. She wasn't pulling back from Caleb—exactly. But she needed to think things over. "We are filming the big scene at two o'clock. If I don't talk with wardrobe now, it will be too late."

"Okay," Caleb nodded, a slight frown marring his brow. "Would you like to come to my place for dinner?"

Since their first date, they had kept their time together private. For two weeks, when not on the set, they had gone on picnics and long walks—away from prying eyes. This was the first time Caleb had invited Callie to his home. She knew he lived in a house in the Hollywood Hills. In truth, she was dying to know what it looked like. However, she wondered if it would be a mistake.

"Why don't you call me later? I'll let you know then."

"Is something wrong?" Caleb touched her for the first time, taking her arm when she would have walked away. "Your eyes usually tell me what you're thinking, Callie. Sometimes better than words. Today it's like you are trying to hide from me."

"Nothing is wrong," Callie assured him. How could she explain when she wasn't sure what was happening? "I have my mind on the movie, that's all. I'll talk to you later."

Callie rushed off before Caleb could ask more questions. She knew how it must look to him. Confusing. *Well, join the club.* One second she was enjoying their friendship. The next she was turning it into something serious. It wasn't Caleb's fault. He held her hand. Made her laugh. Callie was the one with the problem. It wasn't fair to project her unfounded fears onto him.

Unfounded. Callie stopped in her tracks. Why was she intent on ruining what she had with Caleb? They were having a good time. That was all. Caleb's main focus was on his career. It was one of the things they had in common. He didn't have time for a serious relationship. Neither did Callie. It made them the perfect couple—so to speak.

Calling herself all kinds of a fool, she turned, retracing her steps.

"Caleb?" Callie called out, relieved to see he hadn't gotten far. He stopped, letting her catch up. "Is that invitation still open?"

Slowly, Caleb's smile widened, his eyes warm. The look he gave her made Callie's heart skip a beat. Stubbornly, she blamed it on jogging a whole twenty feet. The accompanying glow she wrote off as the unseasonably warm Los Angeles weather.

"Should I pick you up here?"

"I have some errands to run." Callie felt her heart rate return to normal, but the glow remained. "Outside my apartment? Seven sharp?"

"See you then. And Callie?"

Things settled with Caleb, Callie's mind had already shifted toward the emotional scene she would play that afternoon. Absently, she asked, "Yes?"

"I'm going to kiss you tonight."

Callie sputtered, but she had no response. She was literally speechless. Her response seemed to please Caleb. Chuckling, he held her gaze a second longer. Then, he winked.

Mouth agape, Callie watched his retreating figure. Not only was her brain incapable of forming a single word, it seemed her legs had stopped working. It might have been the first time in recorded history that the mere promise of a kiss turned an intelligent, quick-thinking woman into stone.

Blinking, Callie concentrated on sending a command to her fingers. When they wiggled, she let out a relieved sigh. Raising her hand, she checked her chin for drool. Dry as a bone, thank goodness. At least she had been spared that particular embarrassment.

46

One foot in front of the other, Callie set a path for the wardrobe trailer. Damn Caleb Landis. A kiss was supposed to be spontaneous. How dare he say something so provocative? Out of the blue. With absolutely no warning or fanfare. And to make it sound like it was a done deal. As if she had no say in the matter.

Realizing Caleb's intent, Callie's eyes darkened to the color of storm clouds. Shutting out thoughts of him while the cameras rolled would not be a problem. But before T.K. yelled action and after he called cut, she wouldn't be able to think of anything but Caleb. And he knew it.

Unable to help herself, Callie had to admit that Caleb had played the moment perfectly. Very evil genius with a big dose of sexy thrown in. By the time she reached wardrobe, the storm clouds had lifted from her eyes, the gray cool and deliberate.

Rubbing her hands together, Callie let loose a bit of her own evil genius. If Caleb Landis wanted a kiss, she would give him one he would never forget.

CHAPTER SEVEN

TIPPING HIS HAND might have been a mistake.

As Caleb pulled to a stop outside of Callie's apartment, he was willing to admit that it would have been wiser to let the evening play out, gauge the temperature of the room, then decide if it was time to try for first base.

Deep inside, Caleb had what he called an instigator. A little demon who liked nothing better than pushing people's buttons for the soul purpose of causing trouble. Usually, Caleb had a handle on it. Today was one of those rare occasions when he let the imp loose. And the look on Callie's face—the utter surprise that had entered her gorgeously expressive gray eyes—had been worth whatever backlash he might have to deal with.

Hell, forget the backlash. It was worth it to remind Callie that he was a man. Vital. In his prime. Sexually active. And interested. Of his own free choice, Caleb had entrenched himself in the friend zone. Long walk, intense conversations. Those were nice. He wouldn't trade them for a pot of gold. However, with a firm foundation under them, it was time for a shift.

Nothing seismic. Caleb was already skirting the no fraternization with actresses under his employ rule. Kissing would be a bit of a tightrope walk, but he needed something. From the moment he saw her, Callie had intoxicated his senses. The more he got to know her, the stronger the feeling became. Rehab was not an option. Caleb had made his peace. This addiction was for life.

It was time to start easing Callie into the same mindset. Caleb knew her opinion of long-term relationships. Until she barreled into his life—smart, sexy, and vibrant—he felt the same. Work came first, second, and third. Throw in some fun and games for relaxation. He was young. There was plenty of time to think about a serious relationship. Caleb wanted to settle down, but he thought it was years down the road.

What was the saying? *Life was what happens when you are busy making other plans.* Callie had not been in Caleb's plans. Now that she was here, he wasn't letting go.

Callie bounded down the apartment building steps, jumping into the passenger seat. She wore dark green linen pants, a matching jacket, and a pair of black leather boots. Her hair was slightly damp and smelled like lemons.

"Right on time." Callie gave him an easy smile.

Caleb had considered the possibility that Callie wouldn't be waiting. He hoped he would have had more sense than to pound on her door, demanding that she keep their date. Thankfully, he wouldn't have to find out.

"I spoke to T.K. He's very happy with this afternoon's scene."

"I don't know if this makes any sense, but it was humbling." Callie vibrated with energy. "When the camera started to roll, I found something inside myself that I didn't know existed. I've always believed in my acting ability. This was something else."

Actors had to believe in themselves. If they didn't, nobody else would— especially when they were first starting out. Callie had never come across as arrogant. She was confident, and she knew that she was capable of great things. Hearing the wonder in her voice surprised Caleb. He was sorry he hadn't been there to witness her performance first hand. Luckily, he had the dailies waiting for him in the morning. Before then, he had Callie. With her words and emotions that were so close to the surface, she had the ability to make him feel like he was there.

"Tell me what it was like. What did you feel?"

"Everything." Twisting toward him as far as her seatbelt would allow, Callie laid her hand on Caleb's thigh. It was such a natural gesture—she was so wrapped up in recounting her feelings—he doubted she felt the way his muscles tensed. "I wish it could always be like that. But I'm realistic. This is special. Thank you."

Caleb laid his hand over Callie's, caressing her soft skin with the pad of his thumb. "I'm the one who should be thanking you. You've brought my movie to life." Caleb laughed. "I was reluctant to hire Preston Marsh. Neither of us had worked with him before, but T.K. convinced me the guy had the kind of pretty boy looks we needed. Marsh can be a bit one-note, but working beside you has brought out the best in him."

"Hmm."

Expecting more, Caleb frowned. "You don't agree?"

"I do. Preston is… talented."

They were only a few blocks from his house, smoothly winding through the hills. It felt like it took twice as long as usual to travel the short distance. Caleb impatiently waited until he had pulled to a stop in his garage and turned off the engine before questioning Callie further.

"Do you have a problem with Preston Marsh?"

"Not exactly." Callie unbuckled herself. "I can't wait to tour your house."

"Callie—"

"Let's go inside."

When Callie turned the full power of her gray eyes on him, Caleb felt himself begin to melt. Hell, he was only human. However, he was not a pushover.

"I will have an explanation, Callie." He left the car, waiting until she was by his side before opening the door to the house.

"Over a glass of wine." Callie squeezed his hand.

Caleb flipped on the lights. He liked his house, but it was more of a place to sleep than a real home. The furniture was comfortable, the view of the city spectacular. As Callie wandered around, taking in everything, he was glad he had taken the time to hire a decorator.

This time last year, a visitor would have been hard pressed to tell if he were moving in or out. Boxes sat in the corners, opened but yet to be unpacked. If he needed something, Caleb would rummage through their contents. Sometimes he found the item. More often than not, he would give up and buy another.

Caleb didn't entertain very much. He conducted business at his office or in a restaurant. Having Callie here made him realize that his personal life was sadly impersonal. Work was the center of everything. He took the occasional weekend to get away. Once or twice, he took as much as a week to wind down and refresh his batteries. Sometimes alone, sometimes with the woman of the moment; he would fly off for a spontaneous dinner in Paris or a more structured ski trip to Italy.

Taking a bottle from the refrigerator, Caleb poured two glasses of wine. For five years, he had lived the perfect bachelor's existence. He walked to Callie, handing her a drink, tapping crystal to crystal. What was perfect before had changed. It was time to make his house into a home. With Callie.

"I would live in a tent and do my business in the bushes if I could wake up to that view every morning."

Caleb chuckled. "You paint an interesting picture. How long do you think you could survive without indoor plumbing?"

With a sigh, Callie took a sip of wine. "I do love a hot shower. I suppose I'll have to wait until I can afford a house to go with the view. The way I'm going, I might manage it before the turn of the century."

You could move in with me. Caleb could guess how Callie would receive *that* suggestion. She would be out the door like Roadrunner. And he would have as much luck catching her as sad old Wile E. Coyote.

"After *Meant to Be* hits the theaters, you'll have plenty of money-making opportunities. I suggest foreign language commercials."

"I've heard about those." Callie's eyes lit with interest. "The actor endorses a Japanese beer, pockets a huge check, and nobody in the rest of the world ever sees it."

"Is money that important?"

"Says the man with the multi-million-dollar house." Callie winked, taking the sting and envy from her words. "I want a place of my own. Do you know that I have never lived by myself? That is a luxury I could get used to."

Great, Caleb thought. He practically had her moved in, and Callie's big dream was solitude. Not deterred, he decided the answer was a bigger house. Callie could have all the space she needed to be alone—as long as she shared his bed at night.

"Would you like to sit down?"

Callie took a seat on the sofa. Toeing off her boots, she settled back, sitting cross-legged. Not wanting to crowd her, Caleb took the chair opposite.

"There's plenty of space over here." Callie patted the nearby cushion.

It was tempting. Later, he promised himself. For now, he needed some answers.

"Tell me about Preston Marsh."

"I swear you're worse than a dog with a bone."

Callie ran a hand through her hair, then let out an overly dramatic sigh. It was the first time Caleb could recall her coming close to overacting.

"There are steaks ready to grill and baked potatoes with all the fixings. Not to mention a green salad and garlic bread. None of which will see the light of day until you tell me what I want to know."

51

"Garlic bread?" Callie licked her lips. "That's cruel, Caleb. I haven't come close to a carbohydrate since the day you took me to breakfast."

"You must be joking."

"Don't look at me like that." Callie raised the glass to her lips, then changed her mind, setting the glass aside. "I count calories, like every other woman in Hollywood. You know this business. I hate the double standard, but facts are facts. Chubby actresses are relegated to playing the funny best friend."

Caleb wished he had an argument for that, but what Callie said was sadly true. The days of the fuller-figured leading ladies were a thing of the past. Which was crazy. The world still worshiped Marilyn Monroe. But if she showed up in Hollywood today, she wouldn't get a job until she dropped twenty-five pounds.

"Does that mean you *don't* want any garlic bread?" Caleb teased. As he hoped, Callie smiled.

"One piece. I would take two, but then I would have to jog home."

"One it is."

That settled, Caleb held Callie's gaze, one eyebrow raised. They had a subject on the table that had nothing to do with garlic bread or potential weight gain. Waiting, his fingers tapped out a random rhythm on the arm of his chair. Callie's lids narrowed, the color turning a muddled gray. *That was new*. It wasn't the color of anger, excitement, or happiness. Or any of the myriad of emotions he had seen displayed in her expressive eyes.

"I'm conflicted."

Okay. Conflict equaled muddled gray. Filing that piece of information away, Caleb waited for her to continue.

"It is too late to fire Preston."

It was never too late. Though at this point, it would be expensive and damn inconvenient. No, Caleb wouldn't fire Preston.

"Preston's job is safe," he assured Callie.

"How about bodily harm?" Callie's eyes grew disturbingly pale as she contemplated the idea. "You aren't the violent type, are you? Besides, injuring your leading man would mean a delay."

"Jesus, Callie. What did the bastard do?" Caleb's impatience turned into genuine concern.

"Nothing worth mentioning."

"I could ask Preston."

Callie scoffed. "He won't tell you."

"There are ways to hurt a man that won't show up on camera. Trust me, I can make Preston talk."

Caleb said it in such a way as to leave no doubt in Callie's mind that he was serious.

"Why doesn't that frighten me?" Callie looked perplexed. "I hate violence."

"You know I would only use it as a last resort. And never against somebody weaker. I'm not a hitter, Callie. I am not quick to temper. But if somebody threatens what's mine, I won't hesitate to use whatever tools are at my disposal to stop them."

"Including your fists?" Callie swallowed, her eyes wide.

"As a last resort."

It took a few minutes for Callie to weigh his words. Caleb could almost hear the wheels frantically turning in the clever brain of hers. When he pushed her to open up, he had no idea that this might be a major turning point in their relationship. He chose to go down this road. Now, he had to deal with the consequences.

"Preston has this thing about patting asses. Not just mine. He considers any woman within range to be fair game."

Apparently, Callie decided she could trust him. Steam churned in Caleb's stomach as he listened to her. Taking a deep breath, he tried his best to make certain she didn't regret her choice.

"You should have told me," Caleb said, proud of his casual tone. "Or at least T.K."

"Don't get mad." Callie lowered her gaze. "T.K. witnessed the one and only time Preston was stupid enough to go after my backside."

"And?"

Callie filled him in on the incident, including the promise of silence she extracted from T.K.

"T. K wanted to tell you."

Caleb planned on having a talk with his director. First thing in the morning. Right now, Callie had his full attention.

"That was the last time Marsh moved on you?"

"I informed Preston that if he touched me, or any other member of the crew again, I would have his balls on a platter." Callie made a quick chopping motion. "He agreed."

"Did he keep his word?"

"Don't worry about Preston. Everything is under control."

"Callie." Tired of having to pull the information from her, Caleb joined her on the sofa. Cupping her cheek, he waited until her eyes met his. "Tell me the rest."

"About a week ago. After we had finished shooting the one and only love scene, Preston followed me to my trailer. When I refused to let him inside, he grabbed my arm and tried to kiss me. Big mistake. I kicked him in the shins, and then between the legs. I have no idea how he got to his car, but he crawled all the way to his trailer."

Caleb wanted to yell. He felt like tracking down Preston Marsh and ripping out each of his over-bleached teeth—one by one. He knew things like Callie described happened on movie sets. But not on his.

"Come here." Caleb gathered Callie into his arms. When she burrowed close, he kissed the top of her head. "You *can* take care of yourself."

"That's what I said."

"However, not every woman can. *That* is why you should have told me. What if Preston had gone after somebody else? What if he did more than pat their ass?"

"I couldn't live with myself." Callie pulled back, her eyes wide with distress. "Never again. I promise. I've been so focused on myself, I didn't think. I'm sorry."

"Shh." Caleb smoothed back Callie's hair. She had been lucky. If Preston Marsh had caught her off guard, things might have turned out differently. Marsh was bigger and stronger. A kiss was bad enough. There was no telling what he might have done. "You have three scenes left with the asshole. Is that a problem?"

"No. In one, we barely speak. We argue our way through the other two.

And I get to hurl a paperweight at his head. I'm supposed to miss."

"You don't need my permission to make your aim true." Caleb sighed, his lips curving into a smile when Callie settled back into his arms. "It might not sit well with the police if you take his head off. My advice is to aim lower. Someplace less deadly."

"I've already bruised his balls. Since it is his last scene, maybe a broken foot?"

"I'll leave the details up to you." The woman had a dangerous streak that Caleb approved of wholeheartedly. Smiling to himself, he reminded himself not to get on Callie's bad side.

They stayed that way, wrapped in each other's arms, content to silently watch the twinkling city lights.

"Are you hungry?" Caleb asked. The clock read quarter to eight. "I should start up the grill."

"What about my kiss?"

Caleb hadn't forgotten. His promise to Callie had been in the back of his mind all day.

"Another time."

"Why?" Callie unfastened Caleb's shirt beginning at the bottom. One button, then two, until enough skin was exposed for her hand to rest upon.

"Callie." Caleb swallowed, but he didn't attempt to stop her. "You are entering dangerous territory."

Callie's touch was light, not moving. Yet the heat almost scorched him.

"Tell me why you don't want to kiss me." Callie's words were whispered, her breath caressing his ear.

"That's not what I said." The smart thing would be to move—as far away from Callie as possible. Hell, he had spent most of his life being smart. Caleb opted for something better. Callie, warm and sexy, in his arms. "I thought you might need some time."

"Time? You mean because of Preston." Slowly, Callie shook her head, her soft, fragrant hair brushing against Caleb's cheek. "Nothing happened. I'm pissed, not traumatized."

"I know. I just thought—"

"Caleb," Callie interrupted, her head raising until they were face to face. "I love the sound of your voice. I could listen to you tell me stories all night. But right now?"

Caleb's gaze shifted to Callie's mouth. "Yes?"

"Shut." Her lips brushed his. "Up."

Through the years, Caleb had been called many things. Opinionated. Stubborn. A force to be reckoned with. And he gladly owned up to all of it. However, he had never been called a fool. When Callie deepened the kiss, her arms wrapping around his neck, her fingers threading through his hair, Caleb abandoned any resistance he might have presented. Rational thought—and half-assed arguments—melted away. Callie's warm, soft body pressed against his was what his dreams were made of. Her taste was beyond his imaginings. Sweet, intoxicating.

"You told me this would happen." Callie bit Caleb's earlobe, her tongue failing to bathe away what was more of a jolt than a sting.

"This isn't how I pictured it." With a groan of pure pleasure, Caleb twisted his body until Callie covered him like the best blanket ever.

"Is that a complaint?" She pushed away—just enough so he could see the sparkle in her eyes. Like the sun hitting liquid steel. "Should I stop?"

"Yes." Caleb's arms tightened their grip. "In a minute. Or two."

"Or three?" Relaxing, Callie rubbed her cheek against his.

"Why don't you ask me again in an hour?"

Taking charge, Caleb cut off Callie's laugh. No more feathered brushes, his lips claimed hers, strong and sure and passionate. The kiss was never ending. He loved the sound of her sighs, her gasps—the little moan as he nipped at her lower lip, tugging gently. The slightest pain followed by infinite pleasure.

"I meant to stop at one kiss. I should have known it wouldn't be enough."

"I know what you mean." Callie slid her hand under Caleb's shirt, her fingers caressing the base of his spine. "I've never had a problem stopping before now."

"Does that make me the male equivalent of potato chips?"

"Hmm. Give me a second." Slowly, Callie took a taste of his neck, first with her lips, then her tongue. "Salty." Moving slightly, her teeth closed down on a pulsing tendon. "But you taste so much better."

Caleb was on a dangerous path. A slope that became more and more slippery with each passing second. He knew this was a bad idea, but struggled to remind himself why. They were consenting adults. Unattached. Other than a self-imposed code of ethics he swore he would never break, nobody would suffer if they carried this make-out session to a satisfying conclusion.

Caleb's body ached for Callie. But if that was all he wanted, he could force himself to pull away. This was not a simple itch that he needed to scratch. This was primal. As close to all-consuming as he had ever come. The burning fire raced through his veins. One more kiss—another touch—and the hell with caution. In a few seconds, Caleb wouldn't care what he threw to the wind.

"Tell me to stop."

"Stop." The words were barely more than a whisper. A puff of air against Caleb's overheated skin.

"I need something a bit more aggressive."

Breathing heavily, Callie did as Caleb asked. She stopped, her forehead resting against his shoulder.

"You are my boss."

It wasn't exactly a bucket of ice water drenching his libido, but it was a start. "Go on," Caleb urged.

"I want you." Callie placed a tender kiss on his jaw. "For some time, sleeping with you has felt…"

"Inevitable?"

With a crooked smile, Callie shook her head. "Yes."

"Don't worry." Caleb took Callie's hand, giving it a comforting squeeze. "I find the idea just as terrifying as you do."

"I like you. And I like sex. This should be easy, Caleb. Simple. We can't turn it into something more."

Would that be so bad? Caleb almost said the words, but afraid of Callie's answer, he kept them to himself.

"Let's eat." Caleb cupped Callie's cheek. This time, his kiss was brief and friendly. "About the sex? The day the movie wraps. Save the date."

Callie laughed. "Unless there is some unforeseen delay, our consummation date will be December nineteenth."

Taking her hand, Caleb pulled Callie to her feet.

"I was always good about waiting until Christmas morning to open my presents. For you, I will make an exception."

"Then it's settled. We get naked on the nineteenth."

Caleb watched as Callie opened the refrigerator, whistling as she removed salad fixings. Naked Callie. The anticipation might just kill him. But after kissing her—holding her in his arms—he knew the satisfaction would be worth any wait. Once he had her in his bed, Caleb would work on the next step. Convincing her that what they had together went far beyond sexual attraction.

Caleb wanted to be with Callie for the rest of his life. He hoped that soon, she would feel the same.

CHAPTER EIGHT

ONE DAY CALLIE knew she would look back on the early days of her career and remember the filming of *Meant to Be* with bittersweet fondness. This could wind up as the top—the pinnacle. At the moment, the possibilities looked endless.

On word of mouth alone, Callie's agent had received three offers. Nothing definite—she still had to audition. But the scripts were of such high quality it made her mouth water. Then there was the diversity of characters. The last thing she wanted was to find herself typecast as the pretty leading lady. Callie wasn't afraid to look—or play—ugly. Money and fame would be nice. But she hadn't come to Hollywood to be a movie star.

First and foremost, Callie Flynn was an actress. Hearing the words in her head, she burst out laughing.

"What's the joke?" T.K. plopped down in his director's chair. "I could use a laugh."

After two months of twelve-hour days, Callie felt comfortable enough with her director to share some of her private thoughts. Especially ones that made her look foolish—and more than a bit pretentious.

"If I ever call out that I am an actress in an over-the-top British accent, you have permission to give my ego a firm kick in the butt."

"I'll remember that." T.K. smiled. With a sigh, he rubbed a hand over his stubbly cheek.

"You look tired. Here, take this." Before sitting, Callie had hit the craft services table, grabbing a cup of coffee. From the look of him, T.K. needed it more than she did. "Careful, it's hot."

T.K. took a hefty gulp, making Callie wince. Without blinking, he drank again. Apparently, the director sported an asbestos-coated mouth.

"That hits the spot."

"This is our last day." Callie patted T.K.'s hand. "I know your job isn't over, but give yourself a break. Sleep in tomorrow."

"This has nothing to do with the movie." Rolling his head in a slow circle, T.K. groaned. "I may have met my match. In and out of the bedroom."

T.K. had never struck Callie as the kiss and tell kind of man. She held up her hand, just in case she was wrong. "Spare me the details. Please."

Obviously horrified at the suggestion, T.K. cringed. "God, no. Besides, it would take a month of Sundays to recount my recent adventures."

"I'm not sure what to say. Congratulations?"

"Thank you." Though tired, T.K. looked like the cat who swallowed the canary. "I do have an outside of the bedroom problem if you don't mind lending an ear."

"Sure."

"Nadine Black." T.K. said the name with reverence. "The first time I saw her playing guard dragon outside of Caleb's office, I knew I was in trouble. And after four years, she finally said yes to going out with me on a date. And then another. And another."

"I like Nadine." Caleb's assistant took a little getting used to, but under the prickles rested a heart of pure gold.

"Me too. In fact, I love her."

"That's wonderful, T.K." Though Callie wanted to stay free of such emotions, she was only human. She loved a love story. Knowing the players made it all the more special.

"Do I tell Nadine how I feel?"

"If you wait, do you think it will matter?"

"Maybe." He groaned. "I have no idea. There are times when I catch Nadine looking at me, and I would swear she loves me back. But what if it's indigestion? Or cramps?"

Callie sputtered, her reaction somewhere between humor and disbelief.

"Just so there's no misunderstanding. Are you seriously comparing the look of love to painful menstrual cramping?"

T.K. shrugged.

"Do yourself a favor. Do not mention that to Nadine." Taking pity, Callie reached over, rubbing T.K.'s shoulder. "Tell her how you feel. But don't freak out if she doesn't reciprocate immediately. She might need time to think about her feelings."

"Right." T.K. brightened. "Thank you, Callie. You are wise beyond your years."

"It's only common sense," Callie said but accepted T.K.'s grateful hug.

"Brilliant, I say. Right, Caleb?"

Callie turned her head, her eyes meeting Caleb's. Last night on the phone, he had mentioned that he would stop by the set to watch the filming of the final scene. Though she wasn't surprised to see him, it felt like a month rather than three days. Caleb had been out of town on business. They spoke every day, but it wasn't the same as gazing upon his handsome face. Or looking into those intense blue eyes. Or watching his lips slowly curve into a smile meant just for her.

"Callie's advice is sound," Caleb nodded. "As I recall, I said the same thing last week."

"It sounds different coming from Callie," T.K. said with a shrug. "Smarter."

"You hear that, boss man?" Lips twitching, Callie winked. "I am now the brains. I guess that makes you the beauty." She looked him up and down. "No argument here."

"I won't argue about the brains part." Caleb's blue eyes locked with hers, making his feelings about her beauty clear. And reminding her—as if she could forget—what they would be doing in a few hours.

Callie's heartbeat accelerated. An informal wrap party was planned with the cast and crew that evening at a small bar a few blocks away from the set. After that? Taking a deep, calming breath, Callie firmly pushed any thoughts of sex with Caleb out of her head. She was at work, and she needed her head in the game, not in his bedroom.

"Five minutes, people," T.K.'s assistant director called out. "Callie and Maurice. Front and center."

Without a word, Callie stood, moving onto the set without sparing Caleb another glance. Unlike the first day of shooting, Caleb had no need to wish her luck. She knew what he was thinking. It was in his body language.

Realizing how close she and Caleb had become, Callie felt a brief moment of unease. It had happened so quickly that it snuck up on her without warning.

They were friends. A fact Callie treasured. Since coming to Los Angeles, she had been so focused on her career, she hadn't had a lot of time to make anything but business connections. Her roommates were fellow actresses. Not only were they often in competition for the same parts, they had clashing personalities. Finding somebody who had similar interests and beliefs wasn't easy no matter one's profession. In Hollywood, where everybody moved so fast and were out for number one, it was almost impossible.

Caleb was more than a friend. He was more than her next lover. Callie wasn't certain when it happened. What had started out as fun and light, had morphed into something she couldn't identify. She didn't know if she wanted to. It was safer to pretend they were playing. That they would become lovers, hopefully remaining friends when the passion inevitably cooled.

Without a doubt, Callie wanted Caleb in her life. As a friend and a lover. That was it. No room for more.

"Earth to Callie." T.K. snapped his fingers, drawing her attention back to the here and now. "Don't zone out on me. One more scene. It isn't the most difficult acting job I've asked of you, but it is a pivotal moment. Tessa is telling her father why she is leaving home. We've discussed the motivation. You know your lines?"

Callie nodded.

"You're on the same page as Maurice?"

Maurice Hobart was a journeyman actor. In his mid-fifties, he had been in the business long before Callie drew her first breath. He was known for solid, dependable performances. Playing the part of Tessa's father—a man who felt life had let him down—fit Maurice's slightly lived-in looks perfectly. He and Callie had hit it off immediately, easily falling into their onscreen relationship.

"Let's do it."

Callie took her place. The set was simple. Tessa and her father were in the family kitchen. The square table covered with a faded floral cloth was where they gathered for meals, today it was where they would say goodbye.

For generations, Tessa's people worked the land with little to show for it but a rundown farm and mounting bills. Tired of having nothing and knowing if she stayed, there was nothing for her but marriage to a local boy followed by baby after baby. Tessa wanted more.

The scene was straightforward. Callie tapped into her personal experience of leaving home. Though the situations were very different, she knew how it felt to leave the familiar for the unknown. She spoke with her parents regularly and had visited twice. Tessa would not have that option.

Imagining the pain, Callie dug deep, playing it with the suppressed emotions of a woman who knew in all likelihood she would never see her father again. She grasped Maurice by the hand, not simply reciting words from the script, but feeling them down to her soul. Callie stood, letting the tears that filled her eyes cascade down her cheeks unchecked. With a final look—at her father and her home—she walked away.

"Cut." T.K. called out. "That, ladies and gentlemen, is a wrap."

So much for an easy-peasy scene. Callie felt drained. Something that was supposed to be simple had turned into much more.

Maurice pulled her close, his hug that of a father, echoing the movie. "I don't know what that was," he whispered, his voice catching with emotion. "But I thank the acting gods for letting me be a part of it. If you don't get an Oscar nomination for this, I'll burn my SAG card and hop the first bus back to Mississippi."

Laughing, Callie wiped her face, accepting hugs and compliments from the crew. She wasn't thinking about awards or accolades. So many feelings rushed through her body. Relief. Excitement. She was tired and elated all at once. With so much going on in her brain, she didn't know which way to turn.

"You look dazed." T.K. took Callie's arm, leading her away from the crowd.

"That was…" Callie struggled to verbalize what had no explanation.

"Magic."

"Okay." It was as good a word as any, Callie thought.

"Let Caleb take you to your trailer." T.K. gave her a gentle nudge. "Give yourself a little while to unwind."

Callie was certain she needed to do something, but for the life of her, she had no idea what it was. Caleb was there, taking her hand. Silently, he walked with her, opening the trailer door, guiding her inside.

"Sit."

"I'm not in shock," Callie protested. But she let Caleb settle her in a chair, watching as he took a bottle of wine from the mini-fridge. "I don't want a drink."

"Hot tea? Water?"

"No." Callie felt the lethargy leave her limbs. It was replaced by a surge of power. Pushing to her feet, she crossed the small space, unfastening the row of buttons on her dress. By the time she reached Caleb, the garment hung open to her waist. "I need you. Now."

Caleb let out a slow whistle. Setting aside the wine, his gaze followed the path of Callie's fingers. When the dress hit the ground, she grinned when he let out a groan.

"Callie. Honey. Sweetheart. Don't you want to wait until we have more room? And privacy? Somebody could interrupt us at any second."

Holding up his hands, Caleb backed away, but there was no escape. The trailer was small. When the backs of his knees hit the small bed, he tumbled backward, leaving him exactly where Callie wanted him. She reached over, locking the door, before kicking off her shoes. In nothing but a lacy blue bra and matching panties, she straddled Caleb's thighs. When his hands came to rest on her hips, not to push her away, but pull her closer, Callie smiled with satisfaction. He wanted her as much as she wanted him. The grip of his fingers told the story—as did the heat radiating from his body.

With a sigh, Callie wound her arms around Caleb's neck.

"You can say no." She brushed her mouth against his. "I would never force myself on you."

Threading his fingers through her hair, Caleb cupped Callie's head, his gaze locked with hers as his thumb traced the curve of her bottom lip. Intensely blue, the desire in his eyes took her breath away. "Shut up and kiss me."

Callie was happy to oblige. She wasn't looking for sweet and restrained. This was a long time coming. With the enthusiasm of a starving woman, she held nothing back.

"Why are you wearing so many clothes?" Callie complained when her hands found cloth instead of bare skin.

"I was wondering the same about you."

Before Callie could blink, Caleb unhooked her bra, sending it sailing across the room. He reversed their positions, making her gasp, and like that, her panties were gone.

"What about you? I want—"

"Me first." Caleb dropped to his knees, spreading her legs. Slowly, he ran his hand up the inside of her thigh. "So pretty. Do you taste as good as you look?"

"You tell me."

Grinning, Caleb leaned close, taking a swipe with his tongue. "Mmm. Better than honey."

After that, words were in short supply. Callie gripped the thin blanket, her head falling back, as a gasp of air came bursting from her lungs. She had always enjoyed sex. Not that she had a lot of lovers to compare with Caleb. However, before now, Callie thought the few men she had slept with were better than average. *Wrong!* If she had to grade on a curve, her previous lovers sank to the bottom. Caleb? He soared off the charts into a class all his own.

Speaking of soaring. Callie was close—and in record time. Maybe it was because she hadn't been with a man in months. Or the weeks she had wanted this man with plenty of teasing but no satisfaction. Perhaps, it was simply Caleb and the way he instinctively knew how to touch her. *Where* to touch. Not too hard or too soft. Everything was just right.

Calling out his name, Callie didn't fall into the orgasm, she soared. It wasn't a burst of pleasure, but an explosion. Her body tensed, a fission of electricity sailing over her skin. She couldn't think of any words to describe what was happening, so Callie lay back and let herself feel.

Caleb crawled onto the bed that was barely big enough for her. Lying beside her, he adjusted his big, muscular body until she was draped over his chest, her head resting over his fast-beating heart. "I was going to ask how you were doing, but that smile says it all."

"Are you gloating?" Callie raised one eyelid to check out Caleb's expression. His smile was bigger than hers. "Since I feel so good, I will let it pass—this time."

"It isn't gloating," Caleb corrected. "It's satisfaction over a job well done."

Callie was torn between mild outrage and the desire to laugh. Outrage took too much energy. Chuckling, she shook her head. "You gave me an orgasm. Mind you, it *was* fantastic. But you didn't exactly discover the cure for the common cold."

"Funny," Caleb winked. "I feel like I conquered the world."

Since Callie was still coming down from an amazing high—provided by Caleb—she had no argument. In fact, she felt ready to make him feel even better.

"The world?" When Caleb gave her a smug nod, Callie slid her hand to the bulge between his legs. She unfastened the button at his waist, carefully dragging down the zipper. "Want to go for the universe?"

Caleb took Callie's hand, kissing the palm. Getting to his feet, he stripped in record time. She would have asked him to slow down so she could enjoy the show, but from the way his erection bobbed, it wouldn't have been fair to make him wait. Another time, she promised herself.

"Don't worry about protection. I have a condom." Triumphantly, Caleb took a foil packet from his pants, dropping the garment on the floor.

Callie felt a funny zing in the vicinity of her heart. Though she was on the pill, Caleb's thoughtfulness touched her deeply. Without her asking, he let her know that he wanted to protect her. Like with Preston Marsh. Caleb hadn't made a big fuss, but after Callie told him what happened with her leading man, he increased security on the set. It was one more example of how Caleb cared. Not just about her, but the entire cast.

I could fall for this man, Callie thought. *Hard.* Realizing the road she was heading down, she slammed on the brakes, coming to a screeching halt. The timing was wrong to think about a long-term relationship. She didn't know if the timing would ever be right.

Caleb knelt on the mattress. Big, hard and—for now—all hers. Callie reached for him, her legs going around his hips, her arms drawing him close.

"Are you ready for me?"

Meeting his intense blue gaze, Callie nodded. As Caleb slid into her body, his mouth closing over hers, any thoughts of the future fell away. She didn't know what tomorrow would bring. Tonight—being with Caleb—was all that mattered.

CHAPTER NINE

CALLIE DIDN'T WANT to move. Warm, relaxed, and sated, she had no reason beyond a natural disaster for her to leave the comfort of the big, king-sized bed. Eventually, she would need to use the bathroom. Food might become a necessity. But at the moment, nothing was on her radar that didn't involve Caleb Landis and a pair of the softest sheets it had ever been her pleasure to snuggle under.

Reaching out, Callie frowned when she found herself alone. That wasn't right. For the last three days, Caleb had never been far from touching distance. And rarely out of her sight. With the movie completed, they acted like what they were. Young, healthy, and in the throes of a mutual sexual fascination. They hadn't left Caleb's house since the night of the wrap party.

Smiling, Callie stretched her arms over her head. She had read about marathon sex sessions in those books nobody admitted to reading. However, it seemed more fiction than fact. Who had that kind of stamina? Callie sighed, hugging her pillow close. Caleb Landis, that's who. The man was wonderfully insatiable. In the bed. On the floor. The shower. The sofa. The kitchen counter. Up against the wall. Somewhere in Callie's tired brain was a carefully cataloged list of the places they had sex.

One day—during a sexual dry spell—Callie would entertain herself by scrolling through the many memories. That was for later. Much, much later.

"Good morning."

"It was." Callie sat up, tucking the sheet under her arms more from habit than modesty. Caleb had seen it all—making it clear he liked every inch. "Why are you dressed like that? No. Strike that. Why are you dressed at all? I prefer you naked."

"A little thing called work." Caleb straightened his dark green tie before sitting on the edge of the bed. "I have a meeting that can't be missed. While at the office, I'll catch up on any loose ends that are flying around. If I'm lucky, I will be back around three o'clock."

Forgetting the sheet, Callie wrapped her arms around Caleb's neck. "I can fix dinner."

"No! We can order in."

"Come on. The potatoes were only half burned."

"While the other half was raw. Quite the accomplishment."

Callie would have protested, but Caleb was right. She was a lousy cook. For the sake of their stomachs, takeout was the best option.

"You smell good." Callie breathed in the scent of spice and soap. Plus Caleb. The combination made her senses reel. "Are you sure I can't talk you into staying?"

Laughing, Caleb carefully disengaged Callie's arms. "It wouldn't take much. That's the problem." He stood, putting a safe distance between them. "I'm leaving. Now. But…"

"Yes?"

"I'll miss you."

Callie felt a surge of pleasure. Such a simple sentence, but she knew Caleb meant every single word.

"I'll miss you, too."

Reaching for his jacket, Caleb paused, his gaze narrowing.

"What?" Callie asked.

"Your eyes are purple."

"What?"

"It's true." Caleb peered closer, shaking his head. "Huh. Not anymore, but I swear it's true."

Callie licked her suddenly dry lips. "You must be mistaken. My eyes are gray. Simple as that."

"There is nothing simple about your eyes. The shade varies with your moods. Last night was the first time I noticed that shade—true purple."

"Last night?" Feeling a bit lightheaded, Callie breathed deeply, trying to calm her wildly beating heart.

"I would have mentioned it then, but you distracted me. With your mouth." Caleb, unaware of the turmoil his words caused, brushed a kiss across Callie's forehead. "Three o'clock. I'll call if I'm held up."

The second Caleb left, Callie jumped to her feet. In a flash, she rushed to the bathroom, flipping on the light switch, pushing her face inches from the mirror. Stormy. Unsettled. But definitely gray.

Callie continued to stare, waiting for a magical change, not the least bit surprised when nothing happened. It was a myth. A family legend. There was no proof that her gray eyes would turn purple when she was in love.

Then again, a little voice reminded her, Callie was the first member of her family born with gray eyes in several generations. The last had been Great-Great-Aunt Marigold. A woman Callie had never met.

Absently, Callie turned on the shower. She loved everything about Caleb's house, but the water pressure made her do a happy dance. It said something about her state of mind that she could step under the hot spray without noticing. She went through the motions of washing her hair, lathering her body with the creamy bar of soap, then rinsing off.

How had she let this happen? Shuffling across the hardwood floor, she sank onto the bed. *In love?* Callie searched her heart, hoping to find some mistake. Or at the very least, wallow in denial. The problem was, she had always tried to be brutally honest with herself. Whether it concerned her career or her personal life. It was too late to change a habit of a lifetime—no matter how convenient it would be for her peace of mind.

Callie struggled, searching for a solution. She was too young. Too consumed with her career. Too scared to be in love. What was she going to do? Then it hit her. When faced with a difficult situation, she would do what women had done for centuries. Run home to her mother.

Energized, Callie reached for the phone. She had a plane ticket. Her parents sent her one, hoping she would come home for Christmas. Like every holiday since leaving Iowa, Callie had planned to stay in Los Angeles. Calling the airline, she confirmed a seat on the flight leaving that afternoon. Throwing on her clothes, she gathered up the few items that were strewn around Caleb's house. She was cutting it close, but if she hurried, she had time to pack and make it to the airport.

Caleb. The easy thing would be to leave him a note. Easy and cowardly. Callie debated back and forth. Play chicken or do the right thing. The answer was simple. She may be running away from the man she loved, but she couldn't leave him with a piece of paper covered with hastily applied ink.

Taking a deep breath, Callie picked up the receiver and dialed.

THE HOUSE WAS dark. Unwelcoming. A coldness from corner to corner lurked in every shadow. When Caleb left for the office that morning, he had pictured a very different reception upon his return. Turning on every light didn't help. For three days, the wood and glass structure had started to feel like a home. Callie was gone. So was the warmth—the heart—that her smile and laughter carried with them.

Grabbing a beer from the refrigerator, Caleb tossed his keys onto the kitchen counter. Should he be grateful she called? It wasn't as though Callie gave him a chance to respond. The conversation had been brief and almost entirely one-sided.

"I'm going home for Christmas."

The happiness Caleb felt when he picked up the phone faded. Not even a hello, Callie's words hit him bluntly—like a baseball bat to the chest. He had plans for the holidays. True, he hadn't shared them with Callie, but this was the first time she had hinted about leaving town. Caleb planned on surprising her that evening with tickets to Switzerland. He knew she skied. They would spend their days on the slopes, their nights cuddling and making love in their chalet. A roaring fire. Warmed brandy. A week to relax with no interruptions.

When Caleb made the reservations, it had sounded like bliss. Now, he had a bitter taste in his mouth that no amount of beer could wash away. It wasn't that he had to cancel his plans. Callie deserved to spend time with her family. Caleb had been disappointed, but they had plenty of time after the first of the year for them to take a trip. He would leave the destination up to her. No, he was fine with her going home, it was Callie's tone—what she hadn't said that had tied his stomach into a mass of knots.

Callie sounded like she was saying goodbye.

Gulping down what was left in the bottle, Caleb tossed it with glass-shattering force into the garbage. Moving to the liquor cabinet, he poured a stiff shot of bourbon. What had happened between the time he left Callie and her phone call? She had been so happy. Teasing him, asking him not to go. Now she was gone. On her way to Iowa. Hardly the end of the Earth, but Caleb wondered if she would have a place for him in her life when she returned.

"You didn't mention your plans." Caleb sat in his office, confused by the turn of events.

"I've had the plane ticket for weeks." Callie's tone was casual, but Caleb swore he heard nerves under the surface. "Mom and Dad really want the whole family together."

"I see." The truth was, Caleb was in the dark. "When are you leaving?"

"As soon as I pack. My plane leaves this afternoon."

"Will you be back for New Year's?"

Callie paused. Unconsciously, Caleb found himself leaning forward, waiting for Callie's answer.

"I thought I would stay a few weeks. Maybe a month. My next job doesn't start until the end of January."

"In Mexico," Caleb remembered. Callie would be gone for almost two months. Between the movie shoot and her visit with her family, it didn't sound like she had left any room for him.

"With my career heating up, it made sense to take this time to come home. My agent thinks I will be working steadily from now on."

"Callie—"

"I have to go."

"Are you ending things between us?" It was a question Caleb had never asked a woman, and he couldn't believe he asked it now. Especially to Callie.

"Have a great Christmas, Caleb." Callie's words were rushed, as though she was afraid to stop and think about what she was saying. Or give him a chance to respond. "We'll talk soon. Stay safe."

Stay safe? Three hours later and Caleb was still fuming. Tipping back his head, he swallowed the contents of the glass, the bourbon burning on the way down his throat. It took all of his will not to throw the crystal across the room. Setting it in the sink, Caleb latched onto the almost full bottle of alcohol. Taking a swig, he walked to the bank of windows—to the view that had delighted Callie so much.

Damn her. If he had done something to piss her off, she should have stuck around—had it out with him. Running away never solved anything. Didn't he deserve— Hell, Caleb had no idea what he deserved. He *wanted* Callie. Here. Now. He wanted her forever. It seemed Callie didn't feel the same.

He had picked over her every word, searching for some hidden meaning. *We'll talk soon*? Was he supposed to hold onto a vague promise of soon? He felt like a drowning man clinging to the hope that Callie would throw him a life preserver. There was no guarantee. Until he was going down for the third time?

Fuck that. Caleb hadn't gotten where he was by waiting for things to happen. So what if he loved her? Broken hearts mended—wasn't that an unwritten rule? It would take some time, but Caleb had no problem helping the process along. If Callie Flynn didn't want him, plenty of women did.

Caleb swayed. Frowning, he peered at the bottle, surprised to see it was half empty. That much booze—no matter the quality—was never a good idea on an empty stomach. He had skipped breakfast, forgotten lunch, and had no interest in dinner. The only thing coating his stomach was Kentucky's finest. He never drank alone. Not to excess. Flopping onto the sofa, Caleb decided his inevitable hangover was one more thing to put on Callie's lovely shoulders. He took another drink. In for a penny, in for a pound.

Knowing his brain was about to turn to mush, Caleb made a decision. He would take that trip to Switzerland. Alone. But he wouldn't stay that way for long. Every day a different woman. That's what he needed. Quantity over quality, or something like that. Before long, Callie Flynn would be nothing but a distant memory. It was a plan. A damn good one.

Lurching to his feet, Caleb staggered to the bedroom, falling face first onto the unmade mattress. He was drunk, but not drunk enough. The sheets carried Callie's fragrance. Breathing deeply, Caleb felt his guts twist. Closing his eyes, the last thing he saw before passing out were her eyes. Not a clear, bright gray he expected, but a deep, brilliant purple.

CHAPTER TEN

EVERYTHING ABOUT HOME was wonderfully familiar. From the moment Callie stepped off the plane and into her father's waiting arms, his bearlike hug exactly what she needed, it had been easy for her to fall into old habits. Through the airport, to the parked car, and during the ride to her childhood home, the words flowed from Callie non-stop. Her father, as he always had, smiled indulgently, nodding when necessary.

Growing up, Callie's mother was her true confidant. The person with whom she shared her most personal thoughts. But her father was her sounding board. Any idea or crazy dream, Warren Flynn encouraged his daughter to think big. An adventurer at heart, *he* was the reason she had the courage to leave Iowa for Hollywood. It was wonderful to have so many exciting things to tell him.

"I missed the snow," Callie said, looking out the car window as they pulled onto Liberty Avenue. The sidewalks were freshly shoveled, the houses decorated for the season.

Warren laughed. "What was the last thing you said to me before you left for California? Something about never wanting to see another snowflake?"

"We had been through a brutal winter." Callie smiled, thinking about the girl with the big dreams. Had it really been less than three years? It seemed like longer. "My perspective has changed."

"You acquired a layer of polish." Her father took his hand from the steering wheel long enough to pat Callie's arm. "But I can see my little girl shining from those gray eyes. Though at the moment, I can't see anything behind your fancy movie star sunglasses."

While Warren laughed at his own joke, Callie smiled slightly, grateful for the bright sunlight that prompted her to wear the glasses. Her father's offhanded mention of her eyes brought her back to the real reason she was here. She needed some advice—the motherly variety. Purple irises and Caleb Landis were subjects that would have to wait a little while longer.

The Flynn house was dressed to look its festive best. Strings of colorful lights lined every window. The entrance, flanked by a life-sized Mr. and Mrs.

Santa Claus, had a fresh wreath tied with red velvet ribbon hanging on the door.

Before Callie could do more than breathe in the scent of pine, the door flew open.

"There's my girl."

"Mom."

Enveloped in her mother's arms, Callie felt tears sting her eyes. More than snow or decorations or the house that held so many memories, it was having her parents near that made it feel like she had come home.

"Come in out of the cold." Leigh Flynn drew Callie into the foyer. "Warren," she called out to her husband. "Take Callie's suitcases up to her old room. And don't forget to remove your boots before walking on my clean floors."

"Do I ever forget?" Warren asked as he opened the car's trunk.

"Only all the time," Leigh whispered to Callie with a wink. To her husband, she called out, "Of course not, dear."

It was good to know some things stayed the same. Callie had heard the same exchange for as long as she could remember. The best part was the love and affection she heard in her parents' voices. It never changed—thank goodness.

"You're too thin."

"I know." Callie handed over her coat. "I'm counting on you to fatten me up."

"We'll start with hot chocolate and cookies. I'm making your favorite for dinner."

"Macaroni and cheese?" Callie sighed with delight. Even if she had allowed herself that kind of indulgence while in Los Angeles, it wouldn't have been the same. Nobody could top the ooey gooey goodness of her mother's mac and cheese.

76

"Come to the kitchen." Leigh looped her arm through Callie's. "Tell me everything you've been up to."

"There isn't a lot that you don't already know." Except that Callie thought she was in love—and it was freaking her out.

"Phone calls and letters. It isn't the same as having you here in person. And watching the emotions play across your face."

The same height and build, Leigh Flynn looked more like Callie's sister than her mother. They had always been close. Sitting at the counter, Callie realized just how much she had missed her. In Hollywood, rushing around, it was easy to forget how important family was.

"I'm sorry I haven't visited more often."

"You have a life," Leigh set a steaming mug of cocoa on the counter. Taking Callie's chin in her hand, she smiled. "Not that I haven't missed you. And worried—just a little." Leigh looked closer. "What's wrong?"

"Five minutes." Callie smiled, shaking her head. "What took you so long?"

"I was distracted by the excitement of the moment. One look at those eyes, and I knew."

Callie swallowed. She didn't know whether to laugh or cry. Something told her she would be doing plenty of both in the next few weeks.

"I need your advice."

"Who is he?"

"Am I that transparent?"

"I know my girl." Leigh smoothed her hand over Callie's hair. "You've always had a clear vision of your future. Acting came first. Only one thing could knock those blinders catawampus. Are you in love?"

Callie sipped the cocoa. Her mother never beat around the bush.

"Did you ever meet Aunt Marigold?"

"I did. Once, when I was a little girl. What does that have to do with...?" Leigh's searching gaze met Callie's. "Purple?"

"I think so," Callie said, the sense of gloom and doom not quite as prevalent now that she had her mother near. "I didn't see it, but Caleb—"

"Caleb Landis?" Leigh asked, obviously surprised.

Callie had mentioned Caleb often. But she had left out how personal their relationship had become.

"He said my eyes turned purple. Twice."

"So the myth is a fact. Oh, baby." When Callie sniffled, on the verge of tears, Leigh rushed to gather her close. "It isn't the end of the world. Love is supposed to be a good thing."

"I'm not ready," Callie wailed.

Grabbing a tissue from the box she always kept nearby, Leigh handed it to Callie. "Love happens in its own time. Is Caleb a good man?"

"He is the best man I've ever known."

"Since you grew up with Warren Flynn for a father, that is saying something."

"What am I going to do?"

"Simple. You will finish your hot chocolate. Eat a dozen cookies or so. Then you can help me wrap the last of the presents."

"That sounds good, but what about Caleb?"

"Between the food and festivities, we'll talk." Leigh kissed Callie's cheek. "Time with your family is just what you need."

Her mother was right. When Callie left Los Angeles, it felt like her world was coming apart at the seams. Wiping away the last of her tears, Callie bit into a spicy piece of gingerbread. Maybe the cookie was magic. Or maybe it was simply the familiar process of watching her mother putter around the kitchen.

Whatever the reason, Callie felt herself relax. She didn't know what would happen with Caleb. But that could wait. For now, home was where she needed to be.

CALLIE TOOK A pair of heavy socks from the dresser drawer. Though the house had central heating and she knew there would be a warm, cozy fire burning in the living room, her body was no longer acclimated to December in Iowa. Between the socks, a long-sleeved shirt, and a thick sweater over a pair of jeans, she was ready to face the day without worrying about shivering her way through it.

"Hey, sleepyhead. I have a message."

Pulling her hair back into a ponytail, Callie smiled at her sister. Jenna was two years older. She had arrived yesterday, on break from her senior year at Iowa State. Though Callie was the actress, Jenna could never deliver a line without a dramatic pause for effect.

"Well? Spill it."

"It's a surprise."

"A surprise?"

"Call it an early Christmas gift."

"Come on," Callie urged. "I can tell you're dying to spill the beans."

"Nope." Jenna pushed Callie from her room and down the hall. "But I will say this. I'm more than happy to trade all my presents for this one of yours."

Jenna was the original present hound. Their older sister, Sarah, swore her first words were *gimme, gimme, gimme*. Even if her sister meant it as a joke, that she would even mention the possibility of that kind of trade meant whatever was waiting for Callie had to be good.

"Come on," Jenna urged her along. "You always were a slow poke."

"And you were always too impatient for your own good," Callie countered with good-natured affection.

Laughing as Jenna tugged her into the living room, Callie's smile faded when she saw what—or rather who—was waiting for her.

"Caleb."

"Hello, Callie."

Caleb stood. He seemed taller. Which was crazy. It had only been a few days since Callie had seen him. Dressed in jeans and a plaid button-down shirt, his dark hair slightly mussed, he was so handsome he took her breath away.

"Why don't we leave you and Caleb so you can talk?" Leigh shooed a wary Warren and a grumbling Jenna out of the room.

"Call if you need anything," Warren said to Callie, but his eyes—filled with a protective fatherly warning—were on Caleb. "I'll be in the kitchen."

"I don't think your father likes me."

"He's protective of his girls." Callie's head was reeling, trying to take in the fact that Caleb was here. In Iowa. At her childhood home. It felt a bit surreal. Glancing away, she spied the cups and plate of sweet rolls on the coffee table. "How long have you been here?"

"About half an hour. Along with the treats, your mother served me up a few questions."

"Like why are you here?" It was the first one that popped into Callie's brain.

Caleb shrugged. "I was on my way to Switzerland."

"And decided to make a side trip to Iowa?"

Hearing the incredulity in Callie's voice, a small smile formed on Caleb's lips.

"I've never been. And since you made it sound so interesting—"

"Caleb." Shaking her head, Callie sighed.

"The truth?"

"That would be nice."

"You left me." Caleb snapped his fingers. "Boom. We were happy, then you were gone. I wanted an explanation."

"Wanting to be with my family at Christmas doesn't qualify?" Callie knew it wasn't fair. She had asked Caleb for the truth. But how could she tell him that she loved him? Though now that he was here, standing in front of her, she had an overwhelming desire to blurt out everything. Damn the consequences.

"You're scared."

"What? No. Why would you say that?" Callie didn't like the way Caleb was staring into her eyes. Blinking, she looked away.

"Do you think you can hide your feelings from me? I know your moods, Callie. Look at me." When she shook her head, Caleb's tone softened. "Please."

"I'm not scared." Lifting her chin, Callie stared at Caleb defiantly.

"Dark gray. Anger and fear." That put a frown between his brows. "Why, Callie? What did I do?"

Callie's heart ached when she realized what Caleb was thinking. When she left, it hadn't occurred to her that he might blame himself. That he would think he had done something wrong. The truth was just the opposite. He had done everything right. Why else would she love him?

"Purple." Caleb sounded a bit bemused. "I don't know that one. What does it mean?"

Needing to know, Callie rushed to the antique mirror that hung near the fireplace. She leaned close, her eyes wide. Caleb was right. Purple. A deep, glowing amethyst. Tense, she waited for her stomach to clench with distress. Or her palms to grow clammy. Where was the sense of panic? By now, her eyes should be a stormy gray. Unblinking, Callie stared at her reflection. The color didn't change. Pure purple.

"Well, what do you know?" Callie whispered.

"Callie? What's wrong?"

Slowly, Callie walked across the room until she stood in front of Caleb. This was one of those moments she knew she would never forget. Good or bad. Happiness or heartbreak. It was a turning point. The moment she shed the last vestige of girlhood and planted herself firmly in the adult world. A woman. Strong? Definitely. Independent? Without a doubt. Also, ready to embrace all that life had to offer.

Taking a deep breath, Callie softly said, "Purple means love."

Whatever she expected, it wasn't the sheen of tears that covered Caleb's eyes. Or the whispered, "*Thank God*," before he pulled her into his warm embrace.

"I love you, Callie."

"Thank God," Callie echoed, half sob, half laugh.

Caleb cupped her cheek. The kiss they shared was intensely emotional. Passionate. Filled with longing and relief. Callie clung to him, never wanting to let go.

"I planned this differently. I was going to throw a huge party to celebrate the opening of *Meant to Be*. A big, Hollywood spectacle. Your family would be there. And mine. With all that pomp and pageantry, it seemed like the perfect way to tell you I loved you. How could you resist not saying it back?" Caleb let out a self-deprecating laugh "When you left, that idea blew up in my face."

"I would have hated it."

"I know." Caleb rubbed his cheek against hers. "We'll have the party. But I will always be grateful we had this moment. Just the two of us."

"Away from prying eyes," Callie sighed, her heart impossibly full.

"The only eyes that matter are yours."

When Caleb raised his head, Callie knew what he saw. There was no hiding it now. She didn't want to. She never would.

"I love you." Callie voice was low, just for Caleb's ears. But inside, she was shouting—for the world to hear.

"I'll always know?" There was a touch of wonder in Caleb's intense blue gaze.

"Always." More than an answer, it was a promise.

"I want you to marry me, Callie."

Crazy as it sounded, that hadn't occurred to Callie. She thought they would be together. Eventually, he would ask her to move in with him. But marriage?

"Can't we enjoy each other for now? Someday. Maybe—"

"Give me six months."

Callie thought that was reasonable. "We'll talk about it again in June."

"No. I mean marry me now. In six months, if you decide it isn't what you want, we'll end it."

"I…" Callie tried to wrap her head around Caleb's offbeat proposal. "Six months? What if I'm on the fence? Maybe I like it, maybe I'm not sure?

"Then you can have another six months. Then another six months after that. As long as it takes for you to be as certain as I am." Caleb took her hand, placing it on his chest directly over his beating heart. "I know what I want, Callie. You. Forever."

"Six months?"

Caleb nodded.

"Okay. You have yourself a deal." Callie laughed when Caleb let out a whoop, pulling her into his arms.

"I promise, you will never regret it."

Sinking into Caleb's kiss, Callie hoped he was right. Love was a good place to start. *Six months*. Time would tell if it was enough.

EPILOGUE

THE SOUND OF the front door bursting open broke through Callie's trip into the past. A group of big, laughing men, dressed for a snowy Montana day, stomped their way into the house.

"Hail the returning heroes." Colton Landis called out, pounding his chest. "We came, we saw, we conquered. We fed a ton of cattle."

"Oh, good Lord." Sable burst out laughing. She gave Callie a wink. "How could you, the subtlest of actresses, produced such a ham?"

"Hey." Tossing his coat at his group of brothers, Colt swept his wife into his arms, kissing her soundly. "Take that back."

"Never." Sable squirmed out of his embrace. Placing her hands on her hips, she gave Colt a challenging look. "I stand by my words. What are you going to do about it?"

"I'll show you. As soon as I catch you."

With her specialized Army Ranger training, Sable could have easily outmaneuvered her husband, but getting away wasn't the point. Faking left, she took off to her right. By now, Colt knew her moves. Before she reached the stairs, Colt had her backed into a shadowed corner. Where they stayed, sharing whispers between kisses.

The rest of Callie's men paired up with their women. Garrett and Jade. Nate and Paige. Wyatt scooped his daughter from Callie's lap, giving his mother a hello kiss on the cheek before he joined his wife. Joie, sitting on the overstuffed loveseat, scooted over to make room for Wyatt and their little girl. Happily, Francesca cuddled between her parents, her head resting on Wyatt's shoulder.

"Hello, my love."

"Caleb."

Callie held out her hand. Just as handsome as the day they met, she thought with a contented sigh. The few wrinkles around Caleb's eyes, the touch of gray in his dark, thick hair, didn't change the fact. If anything, the years had only added to his appeal. Callie noticed the way women still looked with interest when he entered a room. She didn't mind. Let them eat their hearts out. He was hers. Always and forever.

When Caleb was settled next to her, his strong arm around her shoulders, she rested her hand on his chest—feeling the beat of his heart. After so many years together, in his arms was still her favorite place to be.

"What have you been up to, my love?" Caleb asked, settling a lingering kiss on her lips.

"This and that. Baking cookies. Decorating the tree. Taking a walk down memory lane."

Caleb laced his fingers with hers. "Care to take me with you?"

"Always. Remember the day we met?"

"Like it was yesterday."

Callie smiled. "I was thinking. Our wedding anniversary is next month. Which means it's time for another six-month checkpoint."

"So it is." She could hear the humor in Caleb's voice. "How are we doing?"

"Better than ever."

"Music to my ears."

"Thirty-seven years." Where had the time gone? Callie wondered. Thankfully, it had been spent with Caleb. "I've decided we are a solid bet as a couple. Instead of six months, let's make it a year."

"If you're sure?" Callie nodded. "Then a year it is. Ah, there it is," Caleb sighed, his smile widening as he looked into her eyes. "Purple."

Callie felt her heart swell. Why had she ever doubted? Putting her lips close to Caleb's ear, she whispered, "Always, my love. Always."

TURING THE PAGE FOR A
SPECIAL BONUS BOOK

IF I HAD YOU

CHRISTMAL IN HARPER FALLS

IF I HAD YOU

CHRISTMAS IN HARPER FALLS

CHAPTER ONE

SAM LAUGHTON EASED the rented four-wheel drive Porsche Cayenne onto the turnoff for Harper Falls. The snow was thicker now, cutting his visibility to only a few feet in front of the headlights.

Bad idea to leave Spokane. The car rental guy at the airport warned him of the incoming blizzard. His advice? Get a hotel room for the night. Harper Falls would still be there in the morning.

Instead of a friendly warning, to Sam the man's words sounded like a challenge. He was never one to take the safe way. When someone told him it couldn't or shouldn't be done, Sam barreled recklessly ahead. More often than not proving the naysayers wrong.

Some called it a stubborn streak; others cursed his otherworldly luck. Sam was okay with the stubborn part. As for luck — he made his own. From the time he was a small boy, he knew what he wanted. Money. Lots of it.

Not that he grew up poor. His family had been and still was, proudly middle class. His dad went to work every morning at seven, arrived back home no later than six. Dinner was on the table promptly at six-thirty. Mom happily took care of the house, her husband, and their three children. Look up the word traditional, the Laughton family was the quintessential definition.

Sam adored his parents. They gave him a warm, loving childhood. Even the town he grew up in was right down the middle average. Not too big, not too small.

His brother, Ted, married his high school sweetheart; his sister earned her degree, went back home, and now taught sixth grade at the same school all three Laughton children attended.

Sam admired them all, and visited whenever he could. However, it wasn't for him. He wanted money, glamor, and fame. He'd dreamed of excitement, travel, living in luxury twenty-four seven. And women. He wanted beautiful, sexy women on his arm—in his bed.

Next month he would turn thirty. In the twelve years since leaving home, he hadn't just fulfilled his dreams. He lived a life beyond even his teenage imagination.

Sam made his first fortune as a record producer. Artists sought him out; he was known as a star maker. Then he turned his sights on the movie industry. Untested, he knew no one would give him the artistic control he wanted. Therefore, Sam put up his own money to buy the screen rights to the hottest book in the world. In the right hands, *Wishes* had the potential to be that rare breed, a critical and box office success. Sam believed those hands belonged to him.

Investors weren't exactly lining up to back a first-time producer/director/screenwriter. Sam wasn't discouraged. He sidestepped the usual money resources. He used his considerable charms on anyone who would listen. This was not going to be a cheap production. He only wanted the best. Best locations, best actors, best costumes. Best music. The last item being what brought him to Harper Falls. Rose O'Brian.

Of all the women he knew, she was the only one who could say no with any conviction. She turned down his offer to share his bed. Boy, had that been a surprise. At the time, they were both single, healthy, sexually active adults. He knew that about her because Rose was not a shy little prude. When he asked her to share his bed, she told him in no uncertain terms that she liked sex. Sex with men. She thought he was handsome, and intelligent. Yet she refused. She just didn't want him in that way.

Sam's ego could take a little female rejection. He refused, though, to let her walk away from *Wishes*. Rose argued that she had never done an entire movie score. She didn't think she was right for the job. He didn't agree. In the end, he got his way. Rose's music turned out to be the perfect complement to his vision. If the critics were right, come February, they would both be rewarded with Oscars.

The last time they met in person was at the world premiere of *Wishes*. Rose's big ex-football player future husband acted as her very protective escort. Jack Winston trusted Rose. Sam, he wasn't so sure of.

Before becoming a billionaire security mogul, the guy worked in Hollywood as a bodyguard. Sam could take care of himself in a fight. Jack was bigger, but not by much. Still, when he kissed Rose, it was lips to cheek only.

He didn't want to find out who was tougher; he had a feeling it wasn't him.

Rose half-jokingly invited Sam to spend Christmas in Harper Falls. The invitation was sincere; she just didn't think there was any chance he would accept. She was right. Under normal circumstances, he spent the holidays with his family. If not with them, skiing with friends. He never went away with a lover. This time of year was always about family, and friends. There were eleven other months to feed his voracious libido.

Sam cleared his schedule, ready to depressurize with his family, when word came from his mother that she and his dad wouldn't be home for Christmas this year. An old Army buddy was getting married. Almost sixty years old, this was his first time down the aisle. Sam's parents wanted to share in the holiday-themed ceremony. They were flying to Boston, and staying until after the first of the year.

Colorado skiing was an open choice. Then he remembered Rose's invitation. To be honest, he was intrigued by Harper Falls. What was the allure? From what he understood, the place boasted an array of people even a city ten times the size would be proud of.

Besides Rose, there were her two best friends. Dani Wilde, a Pulitzer Prize-winning photographer, and Tyler Jones, an artist on the rise. Sam even owned one of her sculptures.

Then there were the two billionaires. They brought a massively successful cyber-security company to Harper Falls. Why? They could live any place in the world.

Sam turned onto the main street. Apparently, Harper Falls shut down during major snowstorms. A few lights, from still open businesses, shined through the blizzard with an eerie glow, but there were no other cars to be seen. People wisely stayed home, out of the weather.

According to his GPS, the turn to Rose's house was at the other end of town. Sam had no idea what the condition of the road would be. She lived on a mountain. He looked around, wondering if one of the lighted windows was a hardware store. A set of chains might be needed to get where he was going.

Sam moved along at a snail's pace, his attention on the storefronts, not the road, when out of the corner of his eye he saw a flash of movement. What the hell? Reflexively, he slammed on the brakes, the back end of his car swerving left, and then right before the whole thing came to a stop crosswise in the middle of the road. Thank God for small towns and no traffic.

Sam opened his door, sliding out. He hadn't heard or felt a thump. Nor had he seen any more movement. Fearing the worst, he quickly walked to the other side of the rig. What he saw stopped him in his tracks. No blood. No broken body lying in the snow. Instead, he found a big, wet dog.

Unmoving, man and dog stood for several moments, staring at each other. Sam in amazement. The dog appeared to be unconcerned by the narrowly avoided tragedy he was almost a part of. His head cocked to one side, his mouth open in what could only be called a goofy grin.

He sat waiting. Waiting for what, Sam had no idea.

"You crazy mutt," Sam said, shaking his head. "If I hadn't noticed you at the last second, you would have been roadkill."

Sam knelt, his hand checking the dog's neck for a collar. Nothing. He turned, his blue eyes meeting big, brown ones. The dog leaned nearer, practically begging for a pet. Shaking his head with a chuckle, Sam obliged, smoothing back the wet hair on the big guy's forehead.

"Other than being soaked to the skin, you look like you're in good shape. Well-fed. Did you lose your collar and tags?"

Sam laughed again. Did he think the dog was going to answer? The big animal had intelligent eyes, but he doubted speech was among his talents.

"You go on home now. You've had your little adventure in the snow. I'll bet your owner is worried sick."

The dog gave him one more look before trotting off the road and down the sidewalk. Sam stood, his nose wrinkling at the smell of wet dog on his hand. He picked up some snow, scrubbing off a few hairs and the worst of the scent.

Climbing in the Porsche, Sam noticed colored lights outlining the window directly across from him. *Peony.* Even in the falling snow, he could tell the place would be a cheery haven. The sales clerk might be able to tell him his chances of getting up Crossfire Hill in his four-wheel drive vehicle.

Sam hopped into the cab. Convenient. He could get some information and pick up some flowers. Rose would be his hostess for the next few days. While the gifts he came with were more than adequate, a bouquet was never a bad idea.

Sam parked, turning off the ignition. Getting out of the cab, he didn't notice the big, grinning dog at the end of the block. Sitting. Waiting.

LILA FLEMING KNEW opening the shop on a day like today was an exercise in futility. The streets were deserted. In all likelihood, they would stay that way until tomorrow when the snowplows cleared the roads. Right now, she could be snuggled down on her couch with a cup of hot chocolate and that new mystery she'd meant to read for the last month.

When she spoke to her brother earlier that morning, Alex told her that's what he and Dani were going to be doing. Snuggling that is. Lila was sure that the lovebirds would find something more interactive to do than read a book.

She asked herself, *Why am I standing behind the counter waiting for customers who weren't going to arrive?* Because she was restless, that was why. She felt like something was about to happen, something big. What and when, she had no idea. The waiting drove her crazy.

There was always something to do when you owned your own business. *Peony.* If anyone asked, she always said the shop was what she knew. Back in Oregon, flowers had been the family business. From the time she was old enough to hold a garden hose, she helped water the plants, weed. Later, she graduated to running the cash register.

The sudden death of her mother and father in a plane crash was a shock from which Lila had never recovered. She was in college at the time, Alex in the army. His leave was short, just long enough to arrange the transportation of the bodies from Wyoming, attend the funeral, and jumpstart the sale of the business. At the time, Lila was in no state to take over. She was more than happy not to have the burden.

Sometimes she wondered how she finished school. From the moment she heard about her parents' death, Lila felt like she was walking around in a haze of disbelief. A phone call from Jack Winston was what finally snapped her out of her cloud of gloom.

Jack was her brother's best friend, kindergarten through twelfth grade. Alex joined the Army; Jack went off to play college football. Lila knew they kept in touch. That they talked about her had come as a big surprise. Jack asked her to come to Washington State. He and his business partner, Drew Harper, were moving their company to Harper Falls. It was Drew's hometown; his family founded the place near the turn of the last century. According to Jack, it was a great place to start over.

Lila didn't need much convincing. She needed something new. Something fresh. Flowers were all she knew; it made sense to open a shop. With the help of Jack, Rose, and all their friends, her business thrived from the get go. Last summer when her brother, fresh out of the Army, moved to Harper Falls, everything was perfect. Or rather, it should have been.

It wasn't that Lila was unhappy. She liked her life. Alex was safe, and in love. She had friends. She dated some very nice men. The problem was she once had dreams. Dreams that seemed unimportant after her parents died. Now, four years later, she wondered if maybe she gave up on those dreams too soon.

The bell over the door startled Lila out of her melancholy wanderings. Surprised, she turned to see who was crazy enough to wander out in this weather. She at least had an excuse. Not only did she own *Peony*, she could close up at any time. Her home was above the shop. At the end of her day, no snow boots were required.

"Good afternoon."

"You think? I haven't decided yet."

"Maybe I can help get you there."

Lila turned. She poured hot cider into one of the cups from a set made as a birthday gift for her by Tyler Jones, Harper Falls' resident artistic genius. It was difficult to believe she knew people like Tyler, Rose, and Dani. They were famous, celebrities. Not only could she wave when they passed on the street, they often stopped to talk. They had dinner together, met socially. They were her friends.

"Take this." She handed him the steaming mug. "Nothing bad can happen when you're sipping a hot beverage."

"I never knew cider was magical."

"It isn't." She twisted over the counter, coming back with something in her hand. "Unless you add a cinnamon stick. Now," she plopped it into his cup, "protection complete."

Sam laughed. His eyes sharpened with interest when he finally stopped being annoyed long enough to get a good look at the woman in front of him. Curvy. Oh, he liked curvy. A mass of brown hair streaked with gold and dark eyes shot with just a touch of green. She wasn't tall. Then again, she wasn't short. From where he stood, everything was just right.

"I know you."

"Have we met," he asked, certain he wouldn't have forgotten this beautiful woman.

"Nope."

Puzzled, Sam watched as she walked back behind the counter. *Nice*, he thought, appreciating the way her jeans molded a well-rounded butt. Normally, he was a breast man. When she turned, he couldn't help thinking — JACKPOT. Great ass; spectacularly filled out sweater.

"You *do* know my friend, Rose O'Brian."

He took the magazine from her outstretched hand. There he was, with Rose, at the premiere of *Wishes*. In the background, just to the left, the lovely blonde he'd brought as his date. Sweet Serena. The face of an angel, the mouth of a —.

"High class call girl."

"Pardon me?"

Sam looked at the woman in front of him. Was she a mind reader? If he were the kind of man to pay for his pleasure, Serena would have earned every penny.

"The article next to your picture mentions Hollywood's use of high-priced call girls to seal deals. I wondered if that was true."

95

The look she gave him was wide-eyed, innocent. The sparkle, the twitch of her full lips, told another story. This woman was a tease, in the best sense of the word. He hated when women came on too strong. The excessive compliments, the overly effusive fawning.

Sam liked to laugh. He had a feeling this woman would know just how to make him. He pictured the fun they could have during his brief visit to Harper Falls. Finding a sexy bed partner wasn't on his agenda, but he was flexible. Hopefully, so was she.

"Sam Laughton."

"I know." This time she grinned outright. "It says so right under the picture."

Sam smiled back. Oh, yes. This unexpected holiday just got a whole lot more interesting.

"Will you tell me your name? Or should I just call you gorgeous?"

"No."

"No, you won't tell me your name?"

"No," she clarified. "You can't use any cheesy lines on me. You can flirt. I like that. Save the icky pick-up chatter for when you get back to L.A."

"Paris."

"What?"

"I live in Paris, not L.A."

"Not the point."

"You're right." Lifting a finger, Sam made an x on his chest. "Cross my heart. No cheesy lines. I was serious about the gorgeous part, though. You are. Honestly."

Lila wanted to be cool. Act sophisticated. Not only was Sam Laughton, legendary ladies' man, in her shop, he lived in Paris. And not as in Texas. Her Harper Falls friends may be world travelers, she, on the other hand, was not. Visiting different countries, living in one, was a big part of her set-aside dreams.

"Lila Fleming."

Sam took her proffered hand, shaking it. Normally he would have kissed the back, his eyes locked on hers. Lila, the name suited her, might think such a move *icky*. He needed to rethink his moves. What worked with other women was not for Lila.

"Rose mentioned you were coming to town. I thought I would meet you at the party she and Jack are throwing on Christmas Eve. Having you come into my shop is a surprise."

"A happy one, I hope."

"Are you kidding? I was bored out of my mind. The snow is keeping everyone where they should be — at home."

"Why aren't you? At home," he clarified.

"I live up there." Lila pointed to the stairs in the back of the shop. "I became sick of my own company, even doing inventory sounded good. I was about to start when you came in."

Sam bit his tongue before he told her he couldn't imagine anyone getting sick of her company. Wow, his lines *were* cheesy. He realized he was getting lazy, or maybe his success made it unnecessary for him to dig for anything deeper. He liked women. They deserved more effort on his part. Thank you, Lila. From this moment forward, he planned on being more engaged when he flirted, more thoughtful. Not every woman was the same. This one? Straightforward was definitely the way to go.

"I stopped in to buy some flowers. For Rose."

"That's nice," Lila said. "Most women love getting them."

Most women. But not her, Sam thought. How many unthinking men brought her a bouquet? They would know she worked with flowers all day. She would take them with good grace, of course. Thanking her date, wondering why men had no imagination. What would Lila want? He would have to think about that for a while.

"How did you find me? In this weather, it's a wonder you could see to drive, let alone see my shop, if you weren't familiar with the town."

Lila carried on the conversation with her back to him, her head inside the refrigerated glass case that took up one wall of the shop.

"A dog. He walked in front of my SUV. Luckily, I wasn't going very fast. When I stopped, I was literally facing you."

"That dog?"

Sam looked over at the door to find *that* dog sitting on the other side. He seemed to be waiting. Well, hell.

"I looked for a collar, tags. Nothing."

"If he's lost, the vet might know him. Or he could have a microchip implanted."

Sam looked at the dog. The dog looked back at Sam.

"Where's the vet?" he asked Lila.

Lila put the finishing touches on the box. A pretty red bow, very festive, then handed it to Sam.

"A mixed assortment. Lilies, tulips, even a few roses. The colors are seasonal. As for the vet? She's just down the street. Unfortunately, like everyone else, she isn't there. She will come in for an emergency." Lila looked outside. "He's wet, probably hungry. Not emergency material."

"It is if some kid is missing his dog. Some Christmas."

Sam expected Lila to brush off the idea. So what if a little kid was worried about his dog?

Lila picked up her phone, did a quick search, and then dialed. She talked to someone Sam assumed was the vet, arranging to meet him at her office.

"She'll call as soon as she gets there. In the meantime, we should get that guy in out of the snow."

"I'll do it," Sam stopped her when she would have opened the door. "First, do you have any old towels? The second he's in here, he will be shaking the wet off. Unless you want it all over your shop…?"

"I'll be right back."

Sam didn't have long to wait. Lila was up and down the stairs in a flash, bringing a pile of light yellow towels.

"These don't look very old."

98

"They aren't." Lila shrugged. "But they're all I have. I'd rather wash them instead of my shop."

"Or maybe get new ones?"

"It won't break me," Lila laughed.

She had a great laugh. Natural, a little husky. It made him want to kiss that sexy mouth mid-laugh, catching the joy. Seeing if he would feel what she was feeling.

"Shouldn't we let the dog in?"

Great, Sam thought as he moved to the door. She caught him staring at her mouth. For a guy who prided himself on his smooth, easy manner around women, it was strange how easily this one was shaking his cool.

Cautiously, he opened the door. There was no telling what the dog's reaction was going to be. With his size, his rampaging body could do a lot of damage. He shouldn't have worried. This guy appeared to be a well-trained gentleman. Instead of pushing his way into the shop, he calmly walked in, looked around, continued over to Lila.

"Well, aren't you the gentleman?" she praised when he offered her a paw in welcome.

She knelt, shaking the outstretched foot. Lila didn't recognize him. People walked their dogs past her shop every day. If she'd seen this big, sweet-faced guy, she would remember.

"Let's not take any chances that he's going to remain so well behaved."

Sam took one of the large towels. Starting at the dog's head, he began the considerable job of drying the soaked coat. Lila noticed with pleasure that he was firm but gentle. Sam murmured words of encouragement, praising how well the dog was doing.

So, the big entertainment mogul had a marshmallow center — at least when it came to dogs. It was nice. Her celebrity crush hadn't turned out to be a self-centered jerk.

"There," Sam said, sitting back. "I rubbed the worst of the water off. You'll finish drying naturally in no time."

Sam smiled up at Lila.

"What?" he asked, puzzled by the bemused smile on her face.

"Nothing, really. I was just thinking. Don't you high-powered guys usually hire people to do this kind of thing?"

"Unfortunately, I left my dog dryer home." He winked. "This trip I'm on my own."

"Let me take those dirty towels. I'll hang them out to dry in the back room. Hopefully, I will be able to knock some of that hair off, before I put them in my washing machine."

"Do you have a bowl we can use to give him some water?"

"I do," Lila said as she gathered up the wet towels. "I'll bring it back with me. Won't be a minute."

Sam frowned at her retreating backside. Lila suddenly seemed stiff, a little uncomfortable. What changed while he dried the dog? Where was his sexy, smiling flirt?

"Any theories?" he asked his companion.

No answer came, but Sam took the look in those big, brown eyes to mean, as one man to another, he understood completely. Women could be a mystery.

After quickly dispensing with the towels, Lila took a plastic container she used to scoop potting soil, rinsed it out, and then filled it with fresh water.

What was wrong with her? She wasn't a blushing virgin feeling her first rush of sexual attraction. Sam Laughton was kind to animals. Why should that get her hormones racing faster than usual?

Maybe, because on top of the gentle way he treated the dog, he was outrageously good looking. Tall, the top of Lila's head just skimmed his shoulder. She knew what was under that bulky coat. Just last week *People* ran a whole page, showing Sam and his woman of the moment, enjoying the beaches in some fabulous tropical location. Those pictures showed a man who easily could have been in front of the camera instead of behind it. Broad shoulders, fabulous chest, one of those washboard stomachs that only seem to exist in the movies, or her dreams.

Then there was that face. Holy crap, what a face. Not a pretty boy, Sam Laughton looked like a man. Strong jaw, full lips, and cheekbones that were to die for. How could high cheekbones look rugged? Somehow, he pulled it off.

Lila opened the small fridge she kept in the back. Mostly, it contained water, juice, some diet soda. Nothing to feed a big, she imagined, hungry dog. There was half a sandwich, though. Her assistant left it there the other day.

Meatball sub. Lila didn't think Agnes would mind giving it up, especially when she found out why; she owned two dogs herself.

Reminding herself that for all his shiny glamor, Sam Laughton was just a man. Lila picked up the water and sandwich, and reentered the shop. When he turned, smiling in welcome, she silently scoffed at her own silliness. Just a man? Hardly. At least not like any man she'd ever met.

She set the water down, stepping back away from the spray created by the dog's enthusiastic drinking.

"Wow," she smiled. "He really needed that. I thought he might be hungry. A meatball sub isn't the healthiest option."

She handed the sandwich to Sam.

"It will do in a pinch."

Apparently, the dog agreed. In no time, he ate his snack, drank down another bowl of water, and found a spot just right for a nap.

"Dry, rehydrated — a nice bit of food in his belly. That is one happy dog."

"Animals have simple needs." She looked Sam up and down. "Most animals."

"My needs are simple," Sam assured her. When she snorted in disbelief, he shrugged. Then grinned.

"Relatively simple. I like to be dry. I'm always happiest when my belly has something in it. Water is essential."

"And?"

Oh good, Sam thought, seeing the lovely twinkle back in her eyes. They were reentering the flirt mode.

"If I ask you about your supply of mistletoe, would that be cheesy?"

"No. Not cheesy, just ill timed. There was a big run on it this week. I'm all out."

"None hanging in the shop?"

"I tried that last year. It gave too many men the wrong idea."

"They all wanted a kiss?"

"Most of the guys were fine. It was the others that caused the problem. They wanted to grab any woman within a five-foot-radius. The mistletoe was taken down before closing."

"There are always a few jerks who ruin the fun for everyone else." Sam moved closer. "We could skip the mistletoe."

Lila tried not to smile. He looked so hopeful. That look did wonders for her ego.

"Where's your holiday spirit?"

"Oh, my spirit is just fine." Sam's eyes dropped to her lips.

Not today, fella. Lila was afraid if she let Sam Laughton kiss her, it might end up as a lot more. Her bed was up those stairs. Maybe they would get to the bed. Doing it in her shop wasn't high on her fantasy list, but with Sam, she had the feeling anyplace would be the right place.

"Rose bought a dozen sprigs."

"I don't want to kiss Rose."

Good to know, Lila thought.

"You'll be at the Christmas Eve party tomorrow night. I'll be there."

Sam caught on quickly.

"We're bound to end up under one of those handy mandatory kiss makers. A dozen. Hell, I imagine by the end of the night, we might hit them all."

"Let's not get ahead of ourselves. How do I know you're a good kisser? Maybe you'll think I'm too sloppy."

"Are you?"

"I haven't had any complaints." Lila tilted her head, a questioning look on her face.

"Me?" Sam asked. "I hate to brag…"

"Oh, go on. You know you want to."

"If you insist. The first woman I ever kissed swore I was the best she'd ever had."

"And she was…"

"Twelve. I was a precocious ten."

Lila was fascinated. An insightful, if humorous, look into a young Sam Laughton

"Did this much older woman have a lot to compare you with?"

Sam shrugged. "Let's just say Marcy wasn't the kind of girl who waited for mistletoe."

"A year-round kisser."

"Equal opportunity all the way too. She taught my sister how to kiss."

"Your sister is…"

"A lesbian," Sam told her matter-of-factly. "Olivia wasn't certain at the time. She claims one kiss from Marcy sealed the deal."

"That must be rare."

"Having a lesbian sister?" Sam asked warily. He waited tensely for her to make some offhand homophobic remark. He wanted Lila to be better than that.

"A brother and sister getting their first kiss from the same person. That must be unusual, right?"

Sam relaxed. Sweet. She was so damn sweet.

"I'm not sure it's *Ripley* worthy. A little odd. Definitely anecdotal."

They were close. Close enough to kiss. Close enough to do a lot of things. Lila found herself wanting to give into temptation. Why not? Sam wasn't going to be in Harper Falls very long. When would she get another chance to take advantage of this kind of situation? A real life, bona fide sex god, wanted her. She wasn't naive. This was about more than a kiss. He wanted a holiday fling — with her. She wanted him to have her.

She leaned closer when the phone rang.

"The vet," she said.

Lila was disappointed and relieved all at once. She wasn't ready for Sam Laughton. She wasn't wearing the right underwear. Her body needed primping. Check her legs. Stubble was a no-no. Lotion. The expensive kind she saved for special occasions. So many things. She wanted to make what would be a once in a lifetime experience as close to perfect as possible.

Sam listened as Lila filled the vet in. Damn phone. Lila was about to give him his kiss, he knew it. She wanted more; he could tell. A little Christmas fling. Not what he planned when he accepted Rose's invitation. Lila was a very pleasant surprise.

"She is waiting for you." Lila took a sturdy piece of rope, tying it expertly

103

around the dog's neck. He was very well behaved, but she didn't want to take the chance on him running off between here and the vet's office.

"Nice knot."

"I dated a sailor for about a month. He taught me all kinds of nifty variations."

"Kinky?"

"Studious. He was still learning. I helped." Lila handed Sam the rope. "I don't attract sexually adventurous men. Guys see me as the girl next door."

Sam led the dog to the door. He was halfway out when he turned back.

"Why does everyone underestimate the girl next door?" He gave her a look that said he never would.

"See you tomorrow night," Sam said with a smile. "I'll be looking for you under the mistletoe."

Lila felt her cheeks heat, glad Sam wasn't here to see it. Sometimes she blushed. Not always. It wasn't something she could control or anticipate. Experienced women didn't blush. Did they? She wanted Sam to rip her clothes off in a bout of mad, wild, no holds barred sex. Pink cheeks made men want to take it slow, be gentle. Or back out altogether.

Lila decided right then and there. She wanted one thing for Christmas. Only Sam Laughton could give it to her.

CHAPTER TWO

"THIS IS NOT a permanent situation. Understand?"

Cooper looked at Sam with adoring eyes. They seemed to say, *Think what you like. I'm here to stay.*

"No. I don't have the room, or the time, for a dog. That's final."

The trip to the vet turned out to be a bust. She gave the dog a thorough examination. Like Sam thought, he was healthy, well cared for. Until recently, he must have had a good home. No microchip though.

"He's been neutered."

Even knowing it was for the best, Sam couldn't control a sympathetic wince.

"Men," Dr. Baine smiled, shaking her head. "You all have the same reaction."

"No guy wants to lose his balls, Doctor."

"Mmm." What else could she say? "I can't be sure he's had all his shots. If you want, I can give them to him again."

"Won't that harm him?"

"No," She gave the calm, happy dog a scratch behind his ear. "He would be fine. Better safe than sorry."

"He isn't my dog. There must be someone out there looking for him, right?"

"I don't know him," she said. "It's possible someone passed through town, stopping for some reason. This guy doesn't seem like the runaway type."

Sam swallowed, hating to ask. He looked at the dog, then whispered, "What about the *pound*?"

Even though he spelled it out, he was afraid the dog understood the nasty word.

"Across town. The storm would keep some of the staff away. I'm sure there's a skeleton crew. Want me to call?"

"No," Sam said. It didn't seem right. Especially this time of the year.

"Leave me your contact information. If anyone comes looking for this guy, I'll let you know."

That settled they were now back in the SUV. The road to Rose's house was surprisingly well tended. Freshly plowed, Sam found the trip easy and quick. His companion stretched out in back, unworried.

Could a dog look smug? This one did. Even after the *this isn't permanent* warning. Maybe because Sam gave in concerning the shots. As the vet said, having him vaccinated couldn't hurt. The last thing he needed was the dog getting sick on his watch. That kind of guilt he didn't need.

"I never should have named you."

Sam didn't think it was right to keep calling him dog. He searched for something that suited the big guy, settling on Cooper in honor of his dad's favorite movie star. *High Noon, Pride of the Yankees, Ball of Fire*. He lost count of how many times he and his father would sit watching Gary Cooper. The good, the bad, and the dreadful. Didn't matter. Looking back again, Sam admitted the name fit. The dog somehow looked like a Cooper.

The heavy security gate, down the road from the house, didn't make Sam blink. Jack Winston made his fortune keeping people safe. Why wouldn't he do the same for himself and the woman he loved?

He identified himself; the camera and intercom verified his identity. A few minutes later, he pulled up in front of a house that looked like it was from another century. Nineteenth, if he was any judge. Grandma's house. Homey. Not the kind of place he pictured when he thought about the couple who lived there.

Yet on second thought, the wraparound porch, dark green shutters, bay windows, all screamed Jack and Rose. They were a modern couple. He imagined inside there would be every convenience known to man, or woman. The more traditional outside design was a good choice.

Cooper seemed to know they were at their destination. He sat up, an excited sparkle in his eyes.

"Better than spending your Christmas wandering the streets, right Coop? I understand there's another dog who lives here. Remember. We are guests. I expect you to be on your best behavior and play nice."

As usual, Sam was sure the dog understood every word. Cooper even nodded at him.

"Right. Here we go."

He barely stepped out of the SUV when the front door flew open, a red-haired, streak of energy rushing out. Right behind, Jack Winston.

Sam had just enough time to determine it was a giggling little girl when she surprised him by launching herself at him.

"Charlotte Marie," Jack cried out.

"Don't worry," Sam laughed, scooping her into his arms. "I have a niece about this age. She's always coming at me like that. The Laughton charm acts like a female magnet. Age is no obstacle."

"I appreciate you catching her. She's decided four is a big girl age. That means going outside even when her mother told her not to."

Charlotte, obviously learning how to use her feminine wiles at an early age, batted her eyes at Jack.

"Love me?"

"Always, you little scamp."

He snatched her from Sam, tossing her into the air. The ring of laughter reached the house, drawing a crowd of six women of varying ages.

"Starting a harem?"

"I was blessed with six older sisters, countless nieces, and a mother who could pass for a woman half her age." Jack gave Sam a warning look. "Hands off."

"Your mother, your sisters? Your nieces seem a trifle young. Your soon to be wife?"

"All of the above."

Grinning, Jack tucked his niece under one arm, extending his other. Sam took the hand, giving it a firm shake.

"Thanks for having me, Jack. You look like you have a full house. Are sure I'm not going to be in the way?"

"Go back to your mama, Charlotte." Jack set her down, giving her a gentle pat on the bottom. He waited until she was safely back in the house before turning back to Sam.

"I built this place to accommodate my ever-growing family. If one sister isn't giving birth, another is about to."

"All girls?"

"My dad and I are the only men on the Winston side of the family. Luckily, my sisters all married good men. Who have proceeded to repopulate with girls."

"You don't sound too upset by that."

"Are you kidding?" The big man with sparkling blue eyes gave Sam a friendly pat on the back. "I wouldn't have it any other way. Now, let me grab your bags and get inside where it's loud but warm."

"About that," Sam said as Jack reached for the back passenger-side door. "I brought an unexpected guest."

"So I see."

Cooper greeted both men with a sharp bark. That was a first, Sam thought. Up until now, the dog was virtually silent.

"I know that sound." Jack stood back, his hand making a sweeping gesture towards the snow-covered lawn. "Go on, boy. My yard is your yard."

Cooper leaped from the SUV, running around, rolling in the snow, scoping out the area. Finally, finding just the right tree, he lifted his leg.

"If I'd known he needed to relieve himself, I would have pulled over before we got here."

"Most dogs will hold it until you reach your destination. I take it you haven't had him long."

"It's a long story."

"On cold, snowy days, that's my favorite kind. Looks like your friend is done. Let's go inside. He can meet Edgar; I'll introduce you all around. Then we'll settle down with a hot drink for story time."

Sam took the box that was stamped with a pink *Peony* logo. He waited for Cooper to shake off his newly acquired coat of snow before following Jack inside. What greeted them could only be termed barely controlled chaos. Children ran, played. Parents kept a watchful eye, for the most part, happy to let them.

"What do you think?"

It was so much like the holidays when he was growing up. Sam felt a twinge. If he couldn't be with his own family, this was a nice substitute.

Sam turned to Jack and grinned.

"It feels like home."

LILA PUT AWAY her notes, the regret becoming harder to ignore. She wrote something every day. Sometimes pages, sometimes one line. From a young age, she recorded her thoughts, wrote stories. The only time she stopped was after her parents died. Her mother's encouragement was gone. The loving belief that Lila's dream of being a writer, wiped out in an instant. The muse that used to sit on her shoulder, whispering, was gone.

For a long time, Lila was sure it would never return. As time eased the pain of loss, the spark flickered to life again. Slowly, a bit here and there. Writing became a joy again. The dream of doing it full time was harder to regain. She was a businesswoman. Running *Peony* took all her time and effort. The yellow legal pads stacked in her desk drawer were filled with stories no one would ever see. Now when she wrote, it was no longer with ambition. She wrote because she had to, for herself.

Pushing back from her desk, Lila shut the drawer on her wayward thoughts. She had a party to get ready for. She planned to kiss a very sexy man. Hopefully, more than once. Looking her best was essential.

As a rule, Lila didn't linger in the shower. Tonight, she took her time. She washed and conditioned her long, dark hair. The body wash filled the room with the scent of vanilla. When she finally stepped out, grabbing a fluffy towel, she was smooth and silky from top to bottom.

Drying her hair was always a chore. Most days she didn't bother. A clip to hold it back and she was good to go. With thoughts of Sam floating through her head, she knew that would not do.

Lila pulled out her seldom-used blow dryer before plugging in the curling iron she bought last spring, only to forget about it until tonight. Out of practice, it took some time. When she was done, she stood back, critically examining her work.

Not bad. A little make-up, the right dress. She might not be able to compete with Sam's usual supermodel type, but those women weren't here. She was. Applying her eyeliner, Lila promised herself to do this more often. Why wait for a special occasion? It was easy to forget, in the day-to-day living of life, how good it felt to pamper and primp.

Her choice of what to wear was a no-brainer. In the back of her closet, tags still attached, was a dress. An impulse-buy one day when she was shopping with Rose, Dani, and Tyler.

The soft, jersey knit hugged her body like a dream, highlighting her curves in all the right spots. The forest green color brought out the flecks in her eyes that were exactly the same shade.

Her legs weren't long, but they were shapely. The dress hit her just above the knee showing off her nicely toned calves. Thank you, step class.

Shoes were a problem. In this weather, boots were practical. For tonight, high heels were mandatory. Again, easy decision. Being good friends with the hostess meant Lila wouldn't feel awkward showing up in clunky boots then changing into strappy sandals.

Lila gave herself one more look in the mirror, before heading out. Hair, nice. Makeup? Good — not clown like. Sparkly earrings, her mother's gold bracelet. The dress was a killer. She was as good as she was going to get. Hot. Yes, little Lila Fleming felt ready to seal the deal with Sam Laughton.

They could start with a kiss. She hoped they ended naked, sweaty, and highly satisfied.

"I KNOW YOU didn't expect me to accept your invitation."

Sam stood with Rose, sipping aged malt whiskey. His enjoyment of her home and family grew with each passing hour. The large, open living area was decorated with festive lights, illuminating banisters, mantles, doorways. Boughs of pine scented the room, a large fire crackling, adding to the festive atmosphere. His companion, her shoulder-length brown hair shining with touches of red and gold highlights, glowed brighter than any light. She was lit from within. That's what loving, and being loved in return, will do for you, Sam realized. It made a beautiful woman incandescent.

"No," Rose admitted. "When I invited you, I was certain this was the last place you'd want to be for Christmas."

"Should I apologize? Not only do I show up, I bring an uninvited guest."

Cooper and Edgar, Jack's large black dog of indeterminate breed, were getting along like old friends. A few tentative sniffs was all it took. Now, they were patiently letting three little girls decorate their coats with ribbons of various colors.

"Cooper fits right in. Knowing his story, I'd be mad if you hadn't brought him. As for you, my friend." Rose linked arms with him. "I said I didn't think you would accept. I never would have made the invitation if I didn't want you to."

"Ever regret turning down my many advances?"

"God no."

"Ouch."

Laughing, Rose squeezed his arm.

"I think your ego can take one woman not finding you irresistible."

"Mmm." Sam gave her forehead a friendly kiss. "It did make it easier when I needed to get on your case. If we were lovers, I might have hesitated."

"Ha," Rose said incredulously. "You wanted those songs for your movie. A little intimacy would not have stopped you. You bullied, Sam. Constantly."

"Didn't you write some songs that will live forever? Classics, Rose. *Unconditional* has been number one for two months."

"You don't get to take credit for that, Sam." Looking across the room, Rose's eyes got dreamy. "Jack was the inspiration. You should be thanking him. I know I do. Every day."

"I still say my gentle nudging helped."

"Gentle my…" She did a quick assessment of how many little ears might be around to hear Aunt Rose swear. Too close to call. "My rear end."

Seeing Sam's amused look, she explained.

"Little pitchers have big ears. They also tend to repeat everything I say."

Sam nodded. "Hence, rear end instead of —"

"That goes for you too. Curb the language while you're here."

"Got it. Gosh, dang and shucks only. I promise."

Sam mingled for the next half hour, his eyes constantly checking and rechecking the door. No Lila. He knew she was coming. Earlier when he was talking to Alex Fleming, someone asked about her. She was coming. Being Christmas Eve, she stayed open to catch the last minute shoppers.

"Sam. I didn't know you'd be here."

The enthusiastic slap on his back might have felled a slighter man. As it was, he did stagger forward. Unconcerned, Sam grinned, happy to see the man, no matter how he greeted him.

"Bobby."

At eighty-five, Robert Plank was robust, energetic, and as Sam's shoulder could attest, strong as a bear. His shock of thick gray hair would be the envy of a man half his age. He was friendly, a bit bawdy, and one of the richest men in the world. His money gave Sam the last boost he needed to make *Wishes*. Finding him at a Christmas party in Harper Falls, Washington was a big surprise.

"Thought a young stud like you would be spending the holidays in bed with a beautiful woman. Or two."

The last bit sent Bobby into gales of laughter, drawing smiles from everyone nearby. Bobby had an infectious personality, drawing people in as easily as he made money.

"I would have thought the same about you. Last I heard wife number six was history, making you free to play the field."

"I do like a beautiful woman. Plenty around here. I'm mighty fond of that one in particular."

Sam looked to where Bobby was pointing. Dani Wilde? Really? She was a looker, no doubt. All that white blond hair, her emerald green eyes. Put those together with a shapely body and a face that could grace the cover of magazines. Sam definitely saw the appeal. From their brief conversation, she seemed intelligent, friendly. She was also engaged to Alex Fleming.

"Nothing like that," Bobby assured Sam. "Though I appreciate the thought. No, that sweet lady is like a daughter to me. We met up about four years ago and it was love at first sight. Platonic love. I couldn't be happier that she's found a good man. Unlike me, *that* is a woman who loves once and strong. Lucky for Alex, he feels the same. If I'm too old to kick his ass, I wouldn't hesitate to hire somebody to do it."

"He's pretty hardcore, Bobby."

The older man's usually jovial expression hardened.

"When it comes to those I love, son, so am I."

Sam didn't doubt it for a minute. He shook Bobby's hand before wandering through the crowd. And a crowd it was. Half of Harper Falls must be here. It didn't matter to him that he was a stranger in a group of friends. Sam was a social being. He liked his own company, sometimes nothing else would do. This, though, was where he thrived. He liked people, all types. They liked him back because he was genuinely interested. When someone talked to him, he listened. A talent that came naturally to him.

He particularly liked the company of beautiful women. Rose's friends qualified and then some. When that beautiful woman was also extremely talented, he couldn't resist. Dani Wilde was a respected photographer. Her work was diverse, one time in a glossy fashion magazine, the next a gritty Newsweek feature.

"I wanted to tell you how much I've enjoyed your work over the years."

Dani, her green eyes even more spectacular close up, smiled at Sam.

"I can say the same. Rose complained the whole time she worked with you. I think we can all agree your butting of heads was worth it."

"Now if I could only get her to agree to record for me." Sam leaned in conspiratorially. "She has a voice that would sell a million records. Add to it the way she looks, she would be a superstar."

"Look at her, Sam." Dani tipped her head toward her friend. "She is a superstar without putting herself out in the public eye. She would hate losing her anonymity. The attention she's getting for *Wishes* is bad enough."

"Seems like a terrible waste," Sam said. He hated giving up, even when he knew Dani was right.

"Nobody that happy is wasting anything."

Sam was about to comment when he heard the name he'd been waiting for all evening.

"Lila."

The enthusiastic greeting came from someone in the crowd. Sam wasn't worried about them. His gaze zeroed in on the woman standing near the door. Lila. She took his breath away.

"Oh, no you don't."

Not taking his eyes off Lila's curvy perfection, Sam frowned absently.

"Pardon?"

"Hey." Dani snapped her fingers in front of Sam's face making him lose focus.

"What?"

"Stay away from my future sister-in-law, Sam Laughton," Dani warned. "Your reputation precedes you. Lila is a sweet young woman who doesn't need a wolf sniffing at her door."

"I resent the comparison," Sam said mildly. He glanced back at Lila. Mouthwatering, every inch. "No offense, but how do you know *what* Lila needs?"

"Meaning every woman could use a little of what you have to give?" Dani scoffed.

"Not every woman."

"God save me from the overinflated male ego." Dani took a deep breath then sighed. "I'm sure you would give her a nice whirl, Sam."

"I don't whirl women."

"You know what I mean. Look around." She spread her hands. "There are at least half a dozen unattached women here who would jump at the chance to be your Christmas nookie."

114

"Nookie? Jesus."

"Lila doesn't have the protective gear to withstand your maneuvers. Pick someone else," Dani urged. Her eyes narrowed when she saw Jilly Underwood sauntering over. "Except her."

Sam wasn't interested in the angular blonde bearing down on them, or Dani's reasons for warning him off. Her warnings about Lila were another matter.

"Exactly what do you think I'm going to do?"

He took Dani's arm, skillfully putting a couple dozen people between them and Jilly Underwood. He recognized that predatory glint in her eye and wanted nothing to do with it.

"I'm not saying you would deliberately hurt Lila. You need to understand. She's lived a relatively sheltered life."

"Sheltered as in former nun?"

"Laugh all you want, Sam," Dani told him. "I'm not the only one who will take exception at your interest. Her brother knows how to kill clean and hide the body."

Looking close, Sam realized Dani was only half kidding.

"You think your fiancé is opposed to his sister having some fun."

"Let's just say Alex is protective. If you lived here, had plans to be around, it would be different. Dallying with Lila then skipping out the next day? Not good."

"Dallying and nookie in the same conversation. That's a first."

"I'm serious."

"I can tell," Sam said. That was the problem. What Dani had to say was completely ridiculous, laughable. Unfortunately, he was the only one laughing.

"She is over twenty-one?"

"Yes," Dani sighed, knowing where this was going.

"Fully functioning both mentally and physically?"

"Not the point."

"We can safely assume hymen free?"

Dani gave in. She had to smile, damn him. Too charming for his or Lila's good.

"She has no experience with men who are so... experienced."

Sam could have stated the obvious. So what? If things went according to plan, day after next he would leave town with a very happy memory and Lila would stay — a little more experienced — equally happy. He wasn't worried about her feelings. He knew for a fact, you couldn't break a heart in forty-eight hours.

LILA SAW HIM the moment she entered the house. In her entire life, she had never been so sexually aware of another human being. Pheromones, hormones, good old-fashioned lust. She tingled. Her skin. Inside, outside.

Sam Laughton put every other man in the room to shame. He made her want to do things she'd only read about. She smiled. She was sure he would be an expert at every one of them.

She thought it wise to skirt around him for a little while until she got better control of herself. This was, after all, a family party. *And* her brother was here. Alex was getting better at treating her as an adult. Watching his little sister being sexually aggressive might be more than he would handle.

Instead, she sedately sipped a glass of white wine, chatting with Tyler and Rose.

"Your mother looks lovely tonight, Tyler," Rose said.

Tyler nodded, with a happy look on her face.

"See that hunky guy at the punch bowl?" she asked.

"The tall, slender man with the salt and pepper hair?"

"That's him. Seems the new doctor in town stopped at the beauty shop where mom gives manicures. He was there for a haircut, took one look at her, boom, the rest is history. I would say the man's intentions are definitely honorable."

"How do you know?"

"Because." Tyler gave Lila a wink. "No man hangs around for over a month, not getting any, unless he really cares."

"You're sure they aren't..." Rose searched for a delicate way of putting it.

"Doing the horizontal mambo?" Tyler laughed at the look the other two women gave her. This was her mother after all.

"Mom spent too many years with a man who treated her like crap. She was lonely even when she wasn't alone. If Dr. YumYum can coax her into bed I say more power to him, and way to go, Mom."

Since the topic was already sex, Lila casually asked a few Sam-related questions. Just to satisfy her curiosity. If she was going to sleep with the man, and she was, better to be well informed. She wanted him to leave town with a smile on his face. She wanted to be… memorable.

"I read that Sam Laughton knows a thing or two about pleasing a woman."

"Ha," Rose laughed. "He could write a book. Volumes. Then teach a class using his own source material."

"Then the two of you…"

"Mamboed?" Rose shook her head. "Not me. The women I know who have, are practically legion. They like to talk, why wouldn't I listen? Not one negative review."

"None?" Tyler whistled. "Impressive."

"I know. It doesn't matter how good someone is in bed, he's bound to have one or two dud sessions. Even if it's just a woman with her nose out of joint. Not Sam. He's legendary."

"Good to know," Lila said, her heart rate elevating.

Rose and Tyler exchanged looks. They recognized an interested woman when they saw one.

"Lila, you need to get those thoughts out of your head. Now."

"What thoughts?"

Lila knew she was blushing; the heat in her cheeks was a well-known feeling. Maybe if she ignored her reddening face, so would her friends.

"You can't hide anything with that fair skin." Rose put a comforting arm around her. She wanted to be kind about this while still hitting her point home.

"Sam didn't invent the one-night stand; he just perfected it."

"Before you go any further, let me make something clear."

Lila stood up straighter; annoyed that even at her full height, in heels, both her friends topped her by several inches. To be fair to herself, Rose and Tyler weren't wearing flats.

"I think Sam Laughton is sexy. Who wouldn't? For anything to happen, the attraction has to be mutual." Mentally crossing her fingers, Lila outright lied to her friends. "That doesn't seem likely, does it? I'm wholesome. A glass of milk, if you will. Sam is lobster dipped in butter. Not an appealing combination, is it?"

This time Rose and Tyler didn't need to look at each other. Their thoughts were in perfect sync.

"Grab some water, your pants are on fire," Rose declared.

"Her nose is growing by the second," Tyler agreed.

"What?"

"Lobster and milk? More like sexy man meet sexy woman. Whoosh. Fireworks."

"You think I'm sexy?" Coming from these two women whom she both admired and envied, Lila found it the ultimate compliment.

"Are you kidding?" Tyler looked Lila up and down. "I came to terms with my lack of curves a long time ago. There was a time, my friend, when I would have killed for boobs like yours. Rose has nice ones, Dani's are great, but you, Lila are what straight men salivate over."

"Truth?" Lila decided confiding in her friends was the better way to go.

"Hey." Dani joined their little circle, her green eyes glowing, her cheeks blooming with color. Her lips nicely swollen.

"There," Lila pointed. "It would be obvious to a blind man what Dani and Alex were doing. See her eyes? The little smile on her face? She's been kissed. With purpose."

"Your brother knows his business," Dani admitted, her smile widening.

"No details, please." Lila sighed. "I've never looked like that, felt the kind of heat that sears your insides."

"Ah, Lila." Rose squeezed harder.

"You have. All of you. All the time. You don't need to be having sex to be having sex. I'd bet you anything, Rose, if your eyes met Jack's right now, I could guess what you both were thinking. Sex. When, where, how. The same for Dani and Alex. Tyler has ten years to make up for with Drew. I'm surprised they aren't in an empty room doing it as we speak."

"We aren't that bad."

All three women gave Tyler incredulous looks.

"Ten years *is* a long time."

"I don't blame you a bit," Lila told her. "It simply illustrates my point."

"But Sam…"

"Is the perfect man to help me out of my sexual malaise."

"Good word," Rose conceded. She looked at her two oldest friends, unspoken understanding passing between them.

"We need to get Lila laid. You," she pointed to Dani, "have the hardest assignment."

"Alex?"

"Right."

"Oh, God. Alex."

Her brother and his overprotective instincts did not bode well for her.

"Why does he need to know?"

"Trust me. I'm not going to tell him about his little sister's plans to be debauched by a legendary ladies' man." Dani shuddered at the thought. "If the subject *does* come up, I'll remind him about Portugal. He was a year older than I was, but he was miles ahead in experience. That should give him pause. Alex hates a hypocrite."

"Good." Lila smiled, grateful to her friends for their understanding and help. "Now," she said to Rose. "Please tell me you hung some mistletoe in an out of the way place."

SAM FELT LIKE a teenage boy. It was the last time he remembered sneaking around, desperate for a simple kiss. It was the last time he needed to. Or wanted to.

Here he was in his thirtieth year. He worked hard. Charmed, bulldozed, and hammered his way to the top of an ultra-competitive business. He didn't want his sex life to be difficult. He spent his days pursuing clients, romancing investors.

119

At night, he was happy to sit back and let the women come to him. He liked their company for a few hours. A few weeks at the most. A few tried to manipulate, play hard to get. Sam walked away, no hard feelings. He told himself it was because he didn't have the time. The truth was he didn't find any of them worth the effort. Until now.

Lila. She slipped through the crowded party like an elusive nymph. He knew she was teasing, at times her smile directed at him. He followed, not too close, enjoying the lightness, the fun of the chase. He wasn't going to grab her in front of everyone; she knew that.

They sipped their drinks, made small talk, laughed. All the while staying away from each other. Letting the anticipation build. He was practically giddy. *For a kiss.*

"I thought about a career in the movies. Everyone in Harper Falls says I'm prettier than any of those Hollywood starlets."

He knew the woman, whose name he'd already forgotten, was talking to him. Billy, Tilly. Something like that. Whatever she was saying was lost on him, his concentration focused on Lila, who chose that moment to beckon him with a discreet crook of her finger.

Sam grinned, starting toward the door Lila exited through. He only got a few steps when he felt five sharp claws digging into his arm, his thick cream-colored cashmere sweater providing little protection.

"You really need to remove your nails, lady."

"But..."

Sam didn't speak again, giving her a look that made more than one high-powered producer cower like an inexperienced newcomer. Jilly was no match for the intense blue gaze. She snatched her hand back, watching as Sam crossed the room without a backward glance.

"Want a piece of friendly advice, Jilly?" Seeing the wary expression in her longtime enemy's eyes, Rose smiled reassuringly. "No tricks, no nasty comments, I promise."

"Fine."

"Stop trying so hard. You are an attractive woman; you have money. Let those things work for you."

"You think I should buy a man?"

Rose realized the other woman was considering it. Oh, boy.

"No, Jilly. I think a change of scenery. New blood. Harper Falls has always been too narrow-minded to appreciate your… *unique* brand of charm."

"I do have a cousin in Dallas."

"Texas? All those cowboys and oilmen? Perfect."

"Unique charms?" Dani asked. She and Tyler, after not so discreetly eavesdropping, joined Rose.

"How would you describe them?"

"Nonexistent?" Tyler offered.

"If it gets Jilly out of town, I would tell her she could charm the birds from the trees. I'm tired of her showing up at my parties. She brings down the fun factor exponentially."

"Mmm," Dani shook off thoughts of Jilly Underwood. "Sam has risen in my estimation. He brushed that parasite off without a second thought. If asked, I doubt he could remember her name."

"The way he's been scoping out Lila, I wonder if he knows his own name. Can you feel the sexual chemistry between them?"

"Are you kidding? I thought that last look was going to leave a trail of scorched hardwood."

Rose sighed, linking arms with her friends.

"We are doing the right thing? Backing off, not interfering?"

"She's an adult, Rose." Tyler couldn't keep a touch of worry from creeping into her voice. "He wouldn't hurt her? Physically, I mean."

"God, no. Sam is one of the good guys."

"Enough. I'm officially letting my little chick fly from the nest."

Rose lifted her glass.

"To mind-blowing sex, long may it reign."

"I SEE YOU found some mistletoe."

"I found some mistletoe hidden from public view."

Sam entered the room. An office? Den? Like every other room in the house, there were tasteful touches of the holiday season. Boughs of pine decorated the mantle above the gas fireplace, filling the room with its earthy scent. Lights twinkled in the windows, welcoming those inside and out.

Sam didn't care about any of that. Take away the glitter, the shine. Lila could light up any room with just her smile. Right now, it was turned on him — he was dazzled. He felt an unfamiliar catch in his chest, ignoring it in favor of the feelings she generated in another part of his body.

Lila waited for Sam, letting him cross the room at a slow, almost predatory pace. This was something she had waited for. Not only since their meeting yesterday. Most of her life. A teenage girl, writing flowery love stories about things of which she had no real knowledge. When she was thirteen, all her stories ended with a kiss. This one, she hoped, would go much further. A bed, two naked bodies, afterglow.

She wasn't expecting happily ever after. When Sam left town, she wanted happy memories. Multiple orgasms, please.

"I like that look on your face."

Sam was closer, only a few feet away.

"How do I look?"

"Sexy. I want to eat you, and then go back for a second helping."

Lila laughed, a little surprised by its husky quality. That was new. Like the way Sam made her feel. New — exciting.

"I meant, how am I looking at you?"

This time when Sam spoke, he was closer, right beside her. She could see the silvery sparks in his clear, blue eyes. She noticed a slight stubble coming through the close shave he gave himself earlier. And his scent. Clean, masculine. She wanted to lick his neck, curious if he tasted as good as he smelled.

"You look like you want what I want."

"Tell me," she breathed.

"Us." Sam moved in, his mouth hovering close to her ear. "Naked."

Lila gasped.

"I can feel it. Jesus, I haven't touched you and I know how good it will be."

"I doubt Rose would appreciate us taking advantage of the empty room. You never know when a guest might come in and catch you... decking my halls."

Sam laughed, the heat of his breath sending shivers through her body. His mouth grazed the curve of her ear as he whispered, "You want to trim my tree?"

"Yes."

"Unwrap my package?"

Sam slipped an arm around Lila's waist, his hand running up and down her back. He gave her neck a light, teasing kiss.

"Had enough?"

Lila tipped her head, encouraging his lips to taste.

"Aren't we just starting?"

"Oh, lovely Lila, you have no idea."

Sam kissed along her jaw, her cheek, the corner of that full, tempting, slightly parted mouth.

"I meant Christmas metaphors. Had enough?"

Lila looked up. Sam did the same. Mistletoe.

Without another word, their lips met. Their worlds exploded.

Sam knew how to kiss. He prided himself on his finesse. Not too hard, not too soft. The proper turn of the head, the touch his tongue against his partner's. He didn't thrust; he coaxed. The pleasurable hours he spent perfecting his technique. There was a time to be an animal, kissing a woman was not it. The second his mouth touched Lila's, experience flew out the window. This was primal. Ten seconds in, he knew without a doubt — this was better.

Lila's head swam. This wasn't a kiss. She knew what a kiss felt like. Pleasant, warm. A prelude to pleasant sex with a pleasant man. No, this wasn't anything like that. Sam... possessed her. Took control. Pushed her to someplace she never dreamed existed.

She wasn't worried about bumping noses, or when to breathe. She didn't care if she ever breathed again.

"What are you doing to me?" Sam pulled back, resting his forehead against hers. His breathing was ragged, his heart pounding like a jackhammer.

"Me?" Lila asked, amazed any words were possible. "You did this. I've never... I don't..." Apparently, words were possible, just not coherent ones.

"Together." Sam took her mouth again, making long strokes with his tongue along hers. "Us, combined."

"Yes."

Lila became the aggressor. She didn't want to talk — she couldn't. She didn't want to analyze. This felt too good. Right now, she wanted to feel.

Threading his fingers through her hair, Sam let the kiss go on and on and on. Lila tasted like the headiest wine. Subtle, intoxicating, irresistible. He couldn't stop sipping, taking more until his head spun, his body primed to take the next step. To take her.

"God, Lila."

She needed to touch him, feel the heat of his skin against hers. Sliding her hand under his sweater, her knees weakened. His back was all smooth-skinned muscle. Long, lean. Hot. Her fingers burned as they explored, teasing the waistband of his jeans. Would his butt feel this good? The temptation was too much. One hand ventured under the denim, seeking.

"Stop."

Sam jumped back. He couldn't take any more. One more minute — less. He could have her dress up, her panties down in a heartbeat. There would be no turning back after that. Tempting. He shook his head. No, they weren't doing this here.

"Let's go."

"What?"

Lila looked at her hands, wondering why the palms weren't scorched black. With the sudden removal of all that heat, she felt cold — confused. Go? Go where?

Sam smoothed back her hair. He knew how she felt. His arms felt empty without her, strangely bereft, if that sort of thing was possible. Cautiously, he pulled her close, rubbing his check against the silk of her hair.

"Your place, Lila. Let's go to your place."

"I'm staying with Alex and Dani tonight. Christmas Eve."

"Right." Family. Sam hated messing with that.

"Alex will understand."

Sam chuckled. His libido was under control enough for him to see the humor in her observation.

"Understand that you would rather spend the night having sex with a virtual stranger? I doubt it."

"You're not…"

Lila was going to say he wasn't a stranger. He was. They met just over twenty-four hours ago. Had one conversation. Spent the last ten minutes making out. She *didn't* know him; it only felt like she did.

"Tell you what." Sam straightened her dress, doing the same for his clothes. "Go with your brother. Have a nice Christmas morning. I will call my family, and do the whole present opening thing here."

"All those little girls?" Lila wondered if he knew what was about to come.

"Kids make it special." Sam grinned again. "By noon, I will be ready for a break."

"Me too," Lila said, knowing where he was going. *Hoping.*

"Twelve-thirty, your place. We can take Cooper for a romp in the snow; tire him out. Then spend the rest of the day in bed."

"My bed. You and me." Lila didn't want any loopholes or crossed wires.

"Naked." Sam gave her one more thorough kiss, and then stepped back well out of range.

"Dream of me."

Lila watched Sam leave the room. She lifted her fingers to her mouth. It felt different. She felt different.

Dream of me.

It was funny. Something she could never tell him. Lila was afraid she had been dreaming of Sam Laughton her entire life.

CHAPTER THREE

"MERRY CHRISTMAS, LILA."

"Merry Christmas, Alex."

Lila gave her big brother a hug. It was the first time in years they were spending the holiday together. Alex joined the Army right out of high school. He came home that first year. She remembered laughing at his buzz cut. All his lovely, thick hair gone. He wore it that way for the next ten years, until last spring, when he abruptly left the military. The reasons were still sketchy, at least to Lila. That was fine. She had her brother home, safe and sound. Even his hair was back.

"I thought about getting you a blow dryer," Lila teased, handing Alex his present. "You haven't needed one for so long. Then I realized you can use Dani's."

"Mmm," Alex laughed. His eyes lit up when the love of his life entered the room. "It was high on my list of reasons for asking her to marry me. Now you know, sweetheart. I only want you for your blow dryer."

Dani set down the tray, handing Lila a steaming cup of hot chocolate. The little marshmallows bobbed up and down, slowly melting into the liquid. Yummy.

"I suspected."

Dani settled next to Alex, her hand resting on his leg. It was an intimate gesture, natural, loving. Lila felt an unaccustomed twinge of envy. *Where had that come from?* She didn't want a man long-term. Someday, of course. Not yet. She was only twenty-five. There was plenty of time to find love.

Sam Laughton's face flashed through her brain. What? No. Sam was for fun, nothing more. She was meeting him later. *That* was why she thought of him. Love and Sam did not now, nor would they ever, go together.

"Hey." Alex waved a hand in front of Lila's face. "Earth to Lila. You looked a million miles away. Why are you blushing? What exactly were you thinking about?"

"Nothing in particular," Lila assured him. Her eyes met Dani's knowing gaze, making her blush deepen.

126

"Now I *know* something is going on. You look like a beet. A guilty one."

"I…"

What could she say? *Alex, I'm about to have a brief, torrid affair.* Wouldn't that go over well? She gave Dani a pleading look.

"Alex," Dani said, drawing his attention. "I know from experience that older brothers love to tease. I think this time you might want to give it a pass. Unless you want the details of your sister's sex life."

"What?" Alex exclaimed, obviously horrified at the thought. "No. Absolutely not."

"Then let's finish opening our presents. Mom and Dad are expecting us for a late brunch."

"Are you coming?"

Dani almost choked on her drink, her snort of laughter sending the liquid spilling onto her lap. Alex jumped up to get a towel, leaving the two women alone for a moment.

"After all this, you better be coming," Dani chuckled again. "Over and over and over again."

Lila's blush traveled down her neck. She might be embarrassed, but she was able to join Dani's laughter. Damn straight. She was tired of talking about it. She was ready for Sam Laughton.

COOPER RACED THROUGH the snow, his golden coat gleaming in the sunlight.

Christmas afternoon turned out to be beautiful. Clear blue skies beckoned them with an invitation to play. The man, woman, and dog were happy to comply.

"He loves being out here."

Lila watched as Cooper jumped into a particularly deep drift. He disappeared for an instant before popping back out, shaking off the snow. He checked, making sure Sam was still with him, and then bounded back into the pristine field. The dog left a big, happy trail in his wake.

"He loves being with you."

"I'll admit, he's growing on me," Sam said.

"Does that mean when you go, he goes with you?"

"It means I like him. I don't have room for a dog in my life. I travel too much; my place in Paris is too small." He shook his head with reluctance. "No, Cooper will make someone a great companion. Not me. *You* on the other hand."

Lila thought about it. Cooper would be a lot of work. He would also be a lot of fun.

"Why not?"

"Really?"

"Sure. A woman living alone? I have a security system, state of the art. A dog would be one more layer of protection."

"Then I could visit," Sam ventured. "Both of you."

Lila didn't answer. When he left town that would be it. Lila would not spend her time hoping Sam would find time to pop in for a day or two, leaving for months, even years at a time. They would have today. That was all.

She took Sam's hand, pulling until they fell backward.

"Snow angels."

Sam let Lila change the subject. What was he thinking? Not even out of town and he was hinting about coming back? Crazy. Completely unrealistic. She was right not to answer. They were supposed to have some fun, move on. There was no future. Not for him and Lila.

He flapped his arms and legs, laughing like a kid. Lila did the same. Cooper joined them, alternating between licking one face, then the other. This was what he wanted, Sam reminded himself. Light, easy. No promises. No strings. Not to Cooper. And Lila? He felt that odd clenching around his heart again. Damn it. Especially not to Lila.

"YOU WERE RIGHT about wearing Cooper out. A little water, some kibble. He's out like a light."

An afternoon spent frolicking in the snow left their furry companion happy, and ready for a nap. The corner of her apartment was now his. Lila would get a regular bed later, for now a thick blanket did the job. It was as though Cooper knew he was home. He circled once, twice, before curling into a contented ball. His light snoring followed within minutes.

Lila was too full of anticipation to feel sleepy. Add a few nerves, she decided. Wasn't it only natural? She wanted this; it was going to happen. Sam made her mouth water and her knees weak. He was also much more experienced. She didn't want to be a big, fat disappointment.

Lila could see it now. As Sam wrote his memoirs, thinking back on his many sexual escapades. The best he ever had? Hard to say. A toss-up between that redhead in Monte Carlo and the blonde in St. Tropez. The worst? Easy. That little brunette in Harper Falls.

"What are you thinking?"

Sam stood in front of her, so handsome, so sexy. His dark hair slightly ruffled after removing his knit cap. The sweater he wore, oh boy, could he wear a sweater, was that amazingly soft cashmere again. This time baby blue, almost the exact color of his eyes. Her eyes fell on his smiling mouth, making her thoughts wander. What would he do with those lips? How were they going to feel on her sensitive skin?

"My thoughts are kind of a jumble. All over the map."

"Nervous?" He smiled reassuringly.

"A little."

"Excited?"

"You have no idea."

"I think I do." Sam grazed her mouth with a mere wisp of a kiss. "I feel the same."

"Excited? I believe that. But nervous? Come on."

"I want this to be good for you. Better than good." Sam took her in his arms, swaying to a silent tune.

"There's this little spot, right here." He touched her temple, sliding his finger a little to the left of center. "I want the memory of tonight seared in. You will never forget me, Lila."

Lila stared into Sam's eyes, mesmerized by his words. Thrilled that he wanted to be a part of her — always. He barely touched her and he already had his wish. She would never forget this night.

Not letting her go, Sam bent, and picked up his phone. He tapped a few keys, sending a soft, bluesy melody floating into the room. She smiled. Silly man.

"I don't need romance."

Sam held her gaze, his eyebrows arching up.

"I do."

Sam led Lila into a slow, easy dance. He wasn't lying. He wanted tonight to be different from his usual encounters. Heat, yes. Passion. They were normal. The need for something extra never came into it. Until now. If he ripped the clothes from her body, taking her here with little preamble, it would still be special. Because it was Lila.

"Sam? Is something wrong?"

Yes. She was getting to him. In one afternoon. No, that wasn't right. Lila got to him in the first five minutes. Downstairs in that little shop she made him want her — want more. What it all meant, he didn't want to think about. Not tonight.

"I need to kiss you."

Lila smiled. Bright. Beautiful.

"There's nothing wrong with that."

Standing on tiptoe, she wrapped her arms around his neck, touching her mouth to his. She smiled again when she heard him groan. Her nerves melted and so did she. Luckily, Sam was there to sweep her into his arms.

"I plan on spending the next few hours getting to know every inch of your delectable body." He kissed her again with breathtaking thoroughness. "Any objections?"

"Just one. We have on too many clothes."

"Easiest fix in the world."

Ten long strides had them by her bed. Sam put her down before taking the hem of her shirt.

"Lift your arms."

Lila followed his command. A second later, she stood before him in her favorite red lace bra.

Sam traced the edge of one cup.

"That color makes your skin look like rich, silky cream." He leaned down, his tongue touching the area just above his finger. "Mmm. Sweeter." He tasted again. "Smoother."

Lila swayed. She reached out, frowning when she encountered cloth, not man.

"Take this off. Now."

Sam whipped the sweater over his head, bringing her hands to his bare chest. They both sighed with relief. That was better. He reached around to unfasten her bra, blindly tossing it away. He put an arm around her waist, pulling her until they were pressed together. Then he kissed her again.

It was almost too much. Lila was on sensory overload. Sam's kisses made every other man's attempts seem awkward and immature by comparison. The perfect blend of hard and soft. When his tongue entered, playing a sensuous game of pursue and capture with her own, Lila wondered if she would come from only a kiss. Intense. All consuming. She wanted it to go on forever.

Sam backed her up, pushing gently when her knees hit the mattress. Before she completely settled, her jeans, panties and socks joined her bra, forming a heap on the floor.

"There you go."

He stood back, taking in the view.

Lila wasn't used to being stared at. Especially when she didn't have a stitch of clothing on. *Don't blush*, she begged herself. Not now. Not when every inch of her was open, vulnerable. There would be no hiding it.

As that last thought raced through her mind, Lila felt the telltale heat rush through her cheeks.

"Turn off the lights," she pleaded.

Sam smiled, thinking he understood.

"Are you getting shy on me?"

"No, I…"

Damn, the red was spreading like wildfire. Down her face, her neck, the top of her chest. Think, Lila. Say something before he realized what a hick he was dealing with. Sophisticated, experienced women do not develop full body blushes during sex.

"I don't like looking at naked men."

Lila wanted to slap her forehead. She wanted sophisticated? That was a huge fail. She sounded like an idiot. Why would any woman with half a brain not want to look at a naked Sam Laughton?

Sam paused in the middle of unbuttoning his jeans, a puzzled frown on his face.

"You want the lights out so you don't have to look at my —"

"Thing."

Lila's eyes widened in horror. *Thing?* Cock, damn it. Penis. Dick. She had a grocery list of choices. She picked thing. What was wrong with her? Grabbing the quilt, she pulled it over her body rolling until she was bound tighter than a mummy.

"Lila, honey, what is going on?"

"Nothing." Her voice was muffled but easily understood. "You should go, Sam. I've made a mess of this. Sorry."

Close to tears, Lila waited to hear the sound of Sam's retreating footsteps. Instead, the mattress dipped, his body settling next to hers. No, no, no. Go away. Full blush and tears? She looked like a wet, blotchy, mess. What a turn on.

"It must be hard to breathe in there."

"I'm good."

She heard him chuckle. Now she was a joke? This was getting better and better.

"Lila." She felt Sam pulling the end of the quilt, gently unrolling her. "Come out and tell me what's wrong."

As ridiculous as this had become, Lila couldn't bring herself to crawl out of the hole she'd so awkwardly dug. She clutched at the material, holding on for dear life.

"Why are you still here?"

"Why would I leave?"

"Because I'm a mess." Resigned, Lila dropped the cover from her face. "Look at me. Red from head to toe." She hiccupped. "Wet face, runny nose. A real sexpot."

Deciding this was not the time to laugh, Sam smothered the urge. He gathered the distraught Lila into his arms. Using the end of the quilt, he wiped away her tears then lightly kissed the end of her nose. *Sexpot?* Not at the moment. Just a woman in need of comforting.

"Tell me what happened," he smoothed back her hair. "I thought everything was going great. Did I frighten you? Are you really afraid of seeing my thing?"

"Oh, God." Lila couldn't burrow back under the quilt; so instead, she hid her face in the crook of his neck. "I can't believe I used that word. Penis. I could have said cock or dick."

"All applicable."

"I blush."

"I'm going to need a little more information, honey. You blush. I imagine most people do."

"Sure. Delicate little flushes. I've seen those women. I hate those women." Deciding she might as well get it over with, Lila threw off the last of her cover, revealing her body.

"Look."

"If you insist."

Normally, Sam's exaggerated leer, the way he wiggled his eyebrows, would make her laugh. Right now, she couldn't summon up even the weakest of smiles.

"No, Sam. Really look. I'm red. Top to bottom. Like an over-boiled lobster."

Sam laughed, garnering a horrified look from Lila. When she tried to cover up again, he stopped her.

"Lila." Sam lifted her chin. "Look at me. Please."

When she did, Sam could see the hurt and embarrassment. He felt a little squeeze around his heart. Sympathy and something deeper. Oh boy. He might be in trouble.

"I wasn't laughing at you."

"Why not? I look like a clown."

"I hate clowns. Wouldn't be close to one for anything. You, on the other hand. There is no place I would rather be."

"Right." Lila was not convinced.

"You gave me an out. Did I take it?"

"No. But—"

"I laughed because the idea of me ever finding you anything but hot and sexy is ridiculous."

Sam ran a finger across the bridge of her nose. He lightly caressed her cheek.

"I noticed your blush."

"You'd have to be blind not to," Lila snorted.

He ignored her.

"I watched as it tinged the top of your chest," his fingers followed the path of his words. "Moved to your breasts. Spectacular, by the way. I practically salivated to see if it would reach these wonderfully hard tips."

Without warning, Sam bent to kiss her nipple, his tongue bathing the end with an all too brief taste.

A moan slipped from Lila's mouth.

"You covered up before I found out and now the color has receded," Sam said, disappointed. "Did it get this far? Tell me it did."

"Yes."

Lila breathed the word, her embarrassment fading faster than her blushes. Sam's touch sent sparks flying through her body. The blood rushed from the surface of her skin, moving like molten lava through her veins. She felt an insistent throb between her legs

"Mmm." Sam licked his lips. "I'm sorry I missed that."

"It's splotchy, not sexy."

"You should let me be the judge of sexy, Lila." Sam's kiss left them both breathless. "Remember, I'm the expert."

Remember? Lila was close to forgetting her own name. Sam kissed her again, his lips firm, commanding. She let him take charge, lead her into a sensual world she knew existed but thought she would never be allowed to enter. Sam was the key. He threw open the door. No. More like smashed it to bits. With his battering ram.

Lila giggled. Battering ram. Where had that come from?

"I like that sound. Want to share?"

"I thought of another penis euphemism."

When she told him, Sam laughed so hard he fell back on the mattress, taking Lila with him. He rolled until she was on top, her lovely breasts pressing into his chest. His hands cupped her butt, aligning her just so, and then sat up. Lila's legs automatically circled his hips. The position was perfect.

"My *battering ram* can feel your…What should we call it?"

"Honeypot?"

"Stop," Sam said, laughing uncontrollably. "All this hilarity is causing friction. It feels amazing. Too amazing. I don't want to embarrass myself all over your stomach."

"If that really is a possibility."

"Considering I've been on edge from the moment I met you? Oh, yeah." Sam leaned back. "Now you're blushing again."

"It's a curse."

"I can see how it would be annoying," Sam conceded. "It makes me want to kiss every inch of your pinkening skin. Follow the path as it spreads up and down your luscious body. Then follow back as it slowly fades. I'm going to find ways to make you blush just so I can enjoy the journey."

"Thank you," Lila said softly. She gave Sam the gentlest of kisses.

"I'm serious."

"I know." This time her kiss was deeper. "Thank you."

They stayed that way, looking deep into each other's eyes. Something passed between them in those moments. Deeper than mere attraction. Stronger than lust.

"I want you. Inside me." Lila whispered the words against his mouth. "Can you reach the table by the bed? In the drawer?"

Keeping one arm firmly around her waist, Sam blindly searched. His hand hit the drawer handle, and then he rummaged around inside. When his fingers brushed a familiar foil packet, he smiled against her lips.

"Are you sure this is my size?"

Lila looked at the package, then swiveled her hips, measuring.

"I'll admit when I bought those yesterday, I was using a bit of wishful thinking." She moved again, smiling. "I'd say I was right on the money. Lucky me."

"Size does matter?" Sam asked, expertly rolling on the condom.

"The user matters," Lila qualified, reaching for him — measuring. "Size is a bonus."

"How do you know...?" Sam swallowed. Lila's hand was making pre-coital teasing banter more and more difficult. "You seem certain I know what I'm doing."

"Reputation." Lila breath hissed between her teeth. Sam's magic fingers were probing between her legs. "You have a good one. Rose confirmed."

Wet, Sam thought with satisfaction. He ran two fingers along her opening. Wet and ready.

"How would Rose know?"

"What?" Her brain was turning to mush. "Stop talking, start —"

Lila almost jumped off the bed, Sam's strong arm around her waist the only thing keeping her mattress-bound. What was he doing? Magic fingers? More like unreal. Beyond talented.

"Tell me what Rose said."

"Now?"

"I could stop."

"No!" Was he kidding? "Inside me, please. Then I promise. I will tell you whatever you want to know."

Sounded like a win-win to him. Sam gripped the sides of Lila's hips, lifting her.

"Take my cock. That's right. You know the rest."

Sam took a deep, calming breath. It took an eternity for Lila to position him. He couldn't tell if she was deliberately torturing him or just a little inexperienced at the process. The look of deep concentration on her face made him think the latter. Okay, he could do this. Let her take her time.

His brain searched for the most unpleasant things possible. Anything to keep his mind off her hand on his dick. Let's see. Landfills, curdled milk, Donald Trump. That helped.

"There," Lila said triumphantly.

"Perfect, honey. Take me at your own pace. Don't rush. Slow, easy."

Buoyed by his soft, encouraging tone, Lila used Sam's shoulders to steady herself. The feeling of being in control smoothed out the rest of her nerves. This was what she needed, where she wanted to be. Following his advice, she took him in a bit at a time. Part of her wanted to hurry, get to the good part. Her body knew this was good. Why rush through something that felt close to heaven? She planned on getting there; first, she wanted to savor the journey.

"There," Sam sighed with relief. It hadn't been easy; he gritted his teeth the entire time. Lila's look of accomplishment made it worth it.

"Should I move?"

Sam lifted both hands, cupping her head. His kiss was thorough, letting her know with his tongue what he would soon be doing with his cock.

"Soon."

Sam laughed at her look of frustration. *Trust me*, he wanted to assure her. I *know how you feel*. It was tempting to grab her hips, thrust himself up again. To end this. To fill the aching need he knew was shared by them both. For some reason, he wanted it to last as long as possible. It didn't matter that they had all night. He could take her again and again. This was the first time. Four, five, six more times. What he did *this* time more than any other was how she would remember him. He planned to make it something no other man would ever be able to equal.

"Tell me about your conversation with Rose."

"It would serve you right if I refused."

"Then we both would lose."

Sam cupped her breasts, sighing with happiness. A soft, firm, perfect handful. He rubbed her nipples with his thumbs, causing her to squirm, lifting slightly, and then coming down again on his rock hard erection.

"Careful," he warned, taking a nipple into his mouth. He bit causing her to jump with surprise, not pain.

"Like that?"

"You know I do."

"Then tell me what Rose said and I'll do it again."

Lila growled with frustration. She could tell he was serious. He wanted to talk about Rose while they were... He wanted to talk about Rose.

"Are you hung up on her?"

Sam was busy watching his hands on Lila's breasts. The weight, the way her nipple felt on his palms when he ran them over the hard bud. How dark his tanned skin looked next to the milky whiteness of hers.

"Who? Rose? Why on earth would you think that?"

"You seem awfully interested in what she had to say about you."

Sam's hips thrust up, ever so slightly.

"Don't," Lila moaned. "Not until you answer."

"Rose is getting an awful lot of play."

"My thoughts exactly."

"Fine."

Sam kept his hands on her breasts but raised his eyes to hers. A lot wary, a little turned on. Time to cut the wary altogether. The turned on would grow from there.

"Rose is a beautiful, desirable woman. I invited her to my bed on several occasions. She turned me down flat every time." He kept his gaze steady, easy to read. "I wasn't offended or obsessed. I like her. I'm curious to know if she talked me up or warned you to steer clear."

Believing him, Lila relaxed and smiled.

"Both. The warning came first. When she realized I couldn't be dissuaded, she confirmed the rumors."

"Which are?"

"Come on, Sam. You know what women say about you. Great in bed, generous. Guaranteed orgasms."

Sam was about to say more when Lila moved again. The rest of the conversation could wait. She was expecting an orgasm? It was past time he delivered.

He moved his hands to her hips, his mouth latching onto one of those oh so tempting breasts.

"Sam," Lila cried out, half pleasure, half protest. "I wanted to know about

138

your reputation."

"Time for show, not tell, Lila."

There it was, Sam thought. Her eyes turned liquid gold. Close. They both were. Too much time teasing and talking. He urged her to meet his hips with hers.

"Come with me, Lila."

Sam reached between them, finding the spot that would send her over. There. He heard the change in her breathing, felt her muscles clench around him. Throwing his head back, he shouted her name. A second later, she joined him, his name on her lips.

Movements slowing, milking the last bit of sensation for them both, Sam kissed Lila. Long, slow. The desperation over, he gave her tenderness, holding her close when she collapsed into his arms.

Sam ran a soothing hand up and down Lila's back. How many times had he held a woman just like this? Waited as their heartbeat slowed back to normal? More than he would count. The pleasure blurred as did the faces.

That was how Sam knew. This was different. Lila was different. When he left her bed, she wouldn't become one of many. He'd wanted to make sure she remembered. Now he was caught in a trap of his own making. Not only would he never forget Lila Fleming, he didn't want to.

"YOU SHOULD HAVE told me."

"I wouldn't be telling you now if you hadn't gone all crazy protective brother the second Lila didn't answer her phone."

"Do I have to remind you of all the shit that's gone down lately?" Alex asked. He tried to keep his voice down to a low roar. He wasn't succeeding.

"Of course not."

"Then how is it overreacting when my sister is AWOL?"

"Listen to yourself," Dani said. "This isn't the Army and your sister isn't one of your wayward recruits. She's a grown woman who has the right to a little privacy."

"With that, that..." Alex searched for the perfect word. "Reprobate?"

"Good word," Dani admitted, and then got back to the argument. "She's fine. Lila has spent the night with other men. I don't recall you threatening bodily harm to them."

"That's because I didn't know about it until after the fact." Alex looked at the clock by their bed. "One in the morning. As we speak, they might be," Alex swallowed, "you know."

"I tell you what."

Dani reached over, taking his phone from his tense fingers. She dropped it into the drawer on her side of the bed.

"Instead of worrying about Lila, why don't you show me what people do at this time of the night?"

She kissed him, her hand slipping under the covers.

"Very nice," she said, feeling the length of his growing erection.

"I'm going over there first thing in the morning."

"Mmm," Dani placated with several more kisses. "Maybe wait until ten."

Alex moved his head to the side, giving Dani better access.

"Nine."

Dani smiled. Lifting the covers, she paused, her mouth inches from taking him inside. One swipe of her tongue, his accompanying moan, and she knew she had him. Lila's privacy was safe from her brother's protective prying. And she was in for a very pleasurable night.

CHAPTER FOUR

LILA WHISTLED HER way through her morning work. She was happy. Giddy. And why not? Hours of sexual bliss in the arms of a man who looked like he stepped off the cover of GQ was funny, kind, sweet. There were almost as many laughs as orgasms. And a few tears. They exchanged growing up stories. Telling Sam about the death of her parents was difficult yet surprisingly cathartic. She didn't talk about that time to many people. Her brother — Dani. Rose, and Tyler knew. A close circle of friends. Now Sam.

Lila cried a little. Then he asked her about the good times. No one did that. They always expressed sympathy then moved on from the difficult subject. Sam gave her a chance to remember her parents in the best possible way. Happy — alive. A weight she hadn't been aware of lifted. She felt lighter. Sam gave her that. She gave him another piece of her heart.

Sam proved to be full of all kinds of surprises. He woke her with his mouth. Oral sex had always been a mystery to Lila. She didn't like giving; she never got any pleasure receiving. Until now.

At first, Lila thought she was having the hottest sex dream ever. Sam, doing wicked things to her with his mouth. For the first time, she enjoyed having a man down there. No embarrassment, no awkward tap on the head saying nice try, no cigar. This time, everything was working. His tongue and fingers were in perfect sync, bringing her immeasurable pleasure.

"I'm dreaming," she moaned.

"Me too," a voice answered. "Only in a dream could a woman be so pretty *and* taste like nectar from the gods."

Lila's eyes popped open, a gasp on her lips. *Not a dream.* Sam was… Holy crap. She tried to sit up, move away. The lack of embarrassment her dream provided came rushing in, full force.

"Sam, you have to stop."

"I will," he said, holding her hips steady so she couldn't get away. "Give me another five, ten minutes and I promise to stop."

"But…" Lila moaned, louder than in her dream. Or non-dream. "I don't like that. I mean, I've never gotten any pleasure…What are you doing?"

"Enjoying my pre-breakfast snack."

Lila was too far gone to protest. She laid down, shutting off her mind. The fingers spread through his thick, soft hair, pulling him closer, urging him on. It didn't take even close to five minutes for her to reach that elusive oral sex peak.

When Lila finally became aware of her surroundings, she slowly opened her eyes.

"Sam."

"Mmm."

"Why are you still down there?" She tried to close her legs without any success. Sam's shoulders made it impossible.

"I like the view." His bright blue eyes traveled up her body then back down again. "Beautiful. Too many men don't take the time to enjoy every angle of a woman's body."

"You've seen it all before."

"Every woman is different, Lila," Sam explained, his hand sliding up her stomach over her ribs until he cupped her breast.

"Not *that* different."

"Wrong. The differences are infinite."

Sam scooted up, taking her in his arms.

"Do you know what it takes to be a good lover?"

"Amazing hands, fantastic cock, and talented tongue?"

"No," Sam chuckled. "Though that all helps. Technique is great, I'm all for it."

"Love the technique, big fan."

"Smartass."

"Hey, I'm serious."

"Then let me enlighten you, Grasshopper." Sam laced his fingers with Lila's. He liked the connection. "The secret, after learning the basics, is caring about your partner. When I'm with a woman, my pleasure is magnified when she

142

is enjoying it as much as I am."

"That myth is smashed to bits."

"What myth?"

"The one that says good looking men are often terrible lovers because they don't have to try. Women fall at their feet." Lila cupped Sam's face giving him a long, deep kiss. "You aren't supposed to care if I have fun, as long as you do."

"I thought we established my well-earned reputation as an orgasm machine," Sam joked.

"True," Lila conceded, her eyes twinkling. "You can be the exception to the rule."

"Unique?"

"You like that?"

Sam turned his head and shrugged.

"I've never wanted to be one among many." Sam turned, pushing Lila onto her back. "In the bedroom, my motto is quality *and* quantity."

"Nope."

Lila pushed back. She knew Sam let her, happy to allow her to spread her wings a little and take control.

This time it was Lila who gave Sam's body a long, appreciative once over.

"Well?"

"You'll do."

The truth was Lila didn't know how she wound up in bed with the hottest man on the planet. Not one to look a gift horse in the mouth, she decided not to worry about it — just enjoy.

Part of the fun was finding out she wasn't as vanilla in bed as she always thought. Man on top, woman on bottom. *Boring.* Suddenly, in one night she found herself doing things, having things done to her, she only read about in books. Giving a man a blowjob might not be blindingly original. Or new. But this time, like when he went down on her, she planned to enjoy it.

"Grab the headboard, Sam. I'm about to *blow* your mind."

Now, Lila checked her watch, two short hours later, she could officially say blowjobs were awesome. With the right man.

Lila felt her happiness wane, just a bit. Sam. He was the right man. The man who would walk out of her life today. When she told her friends that her heart couldn't be broken in one day, Lila was right. Not broken — just severely cracked.

"I told you, the cyber campaign needs to be pushed out before the first of the year. I don't care if you're visiting your family. That's why we have computers. Get your ass in gear or you won't have a job to come back to."

Lila's eyes widened. Whomever Sam was talking to, was getting a royal reaming out. If they weren't shaking in their boots, they weren't human.

The mostly one-sided conversation continued in the same vein for several more minutes. Sam's voice getting louder, his language increasingly colorful.

"Hi."

Sam came down the stairs, his hair still damp from his shower. The smile on his face, open, affectionate, showed a completely different man than the one she overheard. This was the Sam she welcomed to her bed. Deep down, Lila knew they were one and the same. That made him what? *An intimate stranger?* A disconcerting thought.

"Is something wrong?"

Sam crossed the room, his arms wrapping around her waist. He gave her the sweetest kiss. *Okay*, she thought, *back to Dr. Jekyll. He must have left Mr. Hyde upstairs.*

"No."

"Yes." Sam tipped her chin up, his eyes concerned. "You look worried."

"You aren't really going to fire that poor person, are you?"

"What person?" Sam frowned. He looked up at the staircase, the light dawning. "You heard that."

"I think all of Harper Falls heard that. You were very… vocal."

"Business."

"*Business*? Is that usual?" she asked warily. "I would hesitate to do business with anyone who talked to me like that."

"I wouldn't blame you." Sam sighed, briefly resting his forehead on hers. When he straightened, his expression was rueful.

"I was talking to Malcolm, my assistant in New York. He had clear, concise instructions. Things that needed to be done before he left for his Christmas holiday."

"I take it Malcolm screwed up."

"He did. I'm in a very fickle business, Lila. What's hot this week is easily forgotten the next. If I say something needs doing, it doesn't mean next week; it meant yesterday."

"*Are* you going to fire him?"

"Not this time." Sighing, Sam pulled her in tight, his hands giving her back a soothing rub. "Contrary to what some might tell you, I'm not unreasonable. I hold my employees up to the same standards I expect from myself. If they're just learning, like Malcolm, they get some slack."

"Just enough to hang themselves?"

"Smartass," Sam chuckled. "No, enough to learn. Malcolm is on strike two. He's been with me for almost a year, Lila. He knows how I work. He's watched me fire people who wouldn't get with the program."

Lila pushed out of Sam's embrace. He couldn't read her expression. Was she that upset by what she had overheard?

"Lila, like I said, it's business. I have no problem shutting it off the rest of the time."

"I know," Lila assured him. "I'm embarrassed."

"Why?"

"Because *your* business is none of mine." She shrugged. "I was startled by what I heard, that's all. I wasn't thinking. I remember Rose once telling me that you could be a trifle... intense about your work."

"Did she?"

Sam smiled. A *trifle* intense? He remembered being a damn hard-ass. He pushed Rose, never letting up. It was his way; he didn't know any other. She wasn't intimidated. She didn't blink. In fact, she gave as good as she got. Turned out to be one of the best experiences of his professional life.

"It doesn't matter, Sam."

"But..."

"Honestly." Lila kissed his cheek, then lingered on his mouth. "You're leaving in a few hours. Let's not talk about your work."

"About that."

"Your work?"

"No," Sam said. He took a deep breath, suddenly less sure. "I want to stay. The rest of the week."

"You do?"

Sam understood the surprise he saw on Lila's face. He felt the same. He took his shower, mentally going over his schedule. Los Angeles for the next few days, a stopover in New York. Paris in time for the New Year. Then he thought of Lila. What would she be doing at midnight on the thirty-first? Who would she be with? Who would she kiss as the clock struck twelve?

It didn't take long for him to figure that one out. She should kiss him.

Why not? He could rearrange meetings. His plans for New Year's Eve were tentative. Several invitations, nothing set in stone.

As Sam rinsed Lila's shampoo from his hair, the scent of her filling the room, he made up his mind. Until now, he hadn't thought about Lila's reaction. Maybe she wouldn't want him to stay. One night might be all she wanted.

"I don't want to push myself on you, Lila. I want to stay; if you'll have me."

Lila didn't know what to say. She left her bed this morning prepared to say goodbye. Resigned. Sam was never meant to be more than one wonderful night. A memory to savor. Suddenly, he offered her a few more days.

Her first impulse was to shout, *YES!* She would take as much of him as she could get. As she opened her mouth to do just that, the words wouldn't come out. By nature, Lila was not an impulsive person. She thought things through. The longer she thought, the more she knew this was a bad idea.

Her heart was already hovering between like and love. Another week with Sam was bound to cement her firmly on the side of love. If she let him walk away now, no harm done. A tinge of regret, that's all. If he stayed, she faced a broken heart for the New Year.

Tell him no, her rational side urged. *No, no, no, no, no.*

Lila looked up at Sam. Sweet, sexy, complicated Sam. In the end, there was only one thing she could say.

"Yes."

"YOU SAID HE was leaving today."

"That's what I understood, Alex." Dani exchanged eye rolls with Rose. "I'm not responsible for Sam Laughton changing his plans."

"One night," Alex grumbled. He gave Jack an accusatory look. "What is it with one-night stands? No one honors them anymore?"

"If you're referring to my one-night stand with Rose —"

"Exactly," Alex exclaimed. "She asked for something very specific. One night, no strings attached. Simple. Traditional. Jack screwed all that up by refusing to give her what she wanted."

"Traditional?" Rose almost choked on her sweet roll. "What is traditional about non-committal sex? And may I remind you, he did give me what I wanted — eventually. My one-night stand turned into forever." She laid her hand on Jack's, the ring he placed there shining bright. "No complaints here."

"Sam Laughton isn't sticking around Harper Falls. No happily ever after for Lila."

The friends were meeting for a post-Christmas breakfast at Harper Falls newest eatery. *Let Them Eat Croissants* followed in the footsteps of other businesses in town. The cuter and punnier, the better. This French patisserie was sandwiched between *Eye Saw You Coming,* an optometrist and *Take Me Out To The Ball Gown,* a shop specializing in formal wear.

Alex was five minutes into his rant, the hot coffee in front of him going cold, his chocolate croissant forgotten. Jack, believing in waste not want not, snatched the roll from his friend's plate, taking a hearty bite.

"There is an age-old covenant," Alex grumbled. "One night means one night."

"Where is that written?" Drew asked. He slapped Tyler's hand when she tried purloining his coffee. "Patience, Ty. The waitress is making the rounds. You can wait thirty seconds for a refill."

Tyler wasn't sure. She needed her morning caffeine. One cup, delicious as it was, didn't cut it. She gave Drew her sweetest *please* smile.

"Fine," Drew sighed. What could he do? He loved this woman. Feeding her addiction came with the territory. He pushed his cup in front of her. His reward? A big, enthusiastic kiss. Who needed coffee? Tyler was enough to jump-start *his* day.

"What is wrong with all of you," Alex demanded. "My sister is in the clutches of a world-famous letch. You're calmly eating pastry and arguing over coffee."

"First," Rose said reasonably. "No one is arguing. Jack *stole* your roll. Drew *gave* Tyler his coffee. Second," she continued before Alex exploded again, "Sam Laughton is not a letch. He likes women. Treats them with respect."

"But —"

"Anything," she continued, "that is going on between him and Lila, is one hundred percent consensual."

"She's right, Alex."

Dani squeezed his hand. She understood why he was worried. All the years Alex was in the Army, he did his part to keep this country safe. It was an important job; one he was good at. Keeping his sister safe wasn't possible. For the first time in ten years, the siblings lived in the same town. Overprotective brother mode came naturally. It was up to Dani and his friends to help him dial it back several notches.

"Lila should be here, with us. Now." Alex looked around the table. "Do you know why she isn't?"

"Because her brother is a pain in her ass she'd rather not deal with?" Jack suggested not so innocently.

Alex gave his old friend a dirty look.

"She's with that, that… *movie producer*."

"I doubt he has her chained to the radiator."

"Really?" Dani turned to Drew. "Why did you have to put that image in his head?"

"That's it." Alex took out his phone. "What's his number?"

Deciding a phone call was better than rushing over to Lila's, Rose pulled up the number on her phone, hitting dial before handing it to Alex.

"What are you going to do?" Dani asked her fiancé warily. When he didn't answer right away, she laid a hand on his arm. "Do not embarrass Lila."

"Don't worry," Alex reassured the love of his life. Unfortunately, his cold, steel smile negated his words. "I'm just going to invite him for a friendly drink."

"At *Tom Tom's*?" Jack asked with a grin.

"At *Tom Tom's*."

CHAPTER FIVE

TOM TOM'S WAS a Harper Falls institution. Opened by a first Gulf War vet, it was considered a rite of passage to have your first legal drink there. If you were underage, you better not sneak in. Tom Unger had a nose for sniffing out a fake I.D. Once caught, you weren't allowed back in, legal or not. Everyone knew the rule. Those who tried to get around it paid the price.

Once a month Tom closed early. Other vets from the area gathered to play poker, air out their personal problems, or simply hang with people who had seen the same kind of hell and lived to talk about it. This was one of those nights.

Sam didn't know any of this when he agreed to have a drink with Lila's brother. That he was going at all, didn't sit well with the lady.

"You don't have to do this," Lila told him after he got off the phone with Alex. "He's treating me like a Victorian virgin. You can't deflower or debauch me."

"No debauching? I'm sorry to hear that."

"Besides," Lila continued, not buying into Sam's attempt at humor, "we only have a few days. This is my time."

"We'll have all night," Sam assured her. "One drink. Two at the most. I charm your brother; assure him I'm as tame as a pussycat. Once I calm his fears, we can enjoy the rest of the week."

"You don't know my brother," Lila told him. "He's a hard-ass when it comes to protecting the women in his life. He sees me as the same girl I was when he left home to join the Army. I've tried. Dani's tried. Nothing can break through that thick skull."

"I can testify; you are all woman."

"Whatever you do, don't even hint that you've seen me naked."

Sam put his arms around her, pulling her close.

"If push comes to shove, I can take care of myself," Sam assured her. "I trained with an expert in Krav Maga."

Between them, Alex, Jack, and Drew were over six-hundred pounds of solid muscle. Lila knew if there were a fight, it would be one on one. Alex wouldn't bring his friends into it. Unfortunately for Sam, Alex alone would be more than enough.

No matter how much *training* Sam had, her brother's experience was garnered out in the field. The desert of Kuwait, the mountains of Afghanistan. She didn't want to hurt his male ego, so she kept quiet. But if push came to shove, Sam would be pushed and shoved into the hospital.

"I can't talk you out of this?"

"Lila." Sam kissed the end of her nose. "Drinks at a local bar. What's the worst that could happen?"

SAM WATCHED AS the lights of Harper Falls faded behind them. *What was the worst that could happen*? Three large men could kill him, dispose of the body, and use each other as alibis. Maybe Lila was right. This was not a good idea.

"Where *is* this place?" he asked Alex. When Lila's brother didn't answer, he turned to the men in the back of the SUV. "I thought Tom Tom's was in Harper Falls."

"Technically, it's outside the city limits," Jack told him. The usually smiling man's face wore an unusually stern expression.

"Sit back," Drew said. "We're almost there."

Ten minutes ago, getting in the big, black SUV seemed like the logical thing to do. No point in taking two rigs, Alex told him.

While Sam greeted Jack and Drew, Lila took Alex aside. He couldn't hear the heated conversation; he could tell it was mostly one sided — Lila's side. She was animated, gesturing, her finger pointing. All the while, Alex stood silently, arms crossed over his massive chest. When Lila finally wound down, without a word, Alex gently patted his sister's shoulder, then kissed her cheek.

"Damn it, Alex," Lila called out as they left the shop. "Behave yourself."

Thinking of that moment, Sam wondered if the little, unconcerned wave he gave Lila as the door closed behind him, was the last time he would see her. It was silly. Alex and his friends were not going to kill him. Beat him up? That was possible. He could take a punch from a normal man. Unfortunately, these guys, with their training, experience, and size, were anything but normal. His big words to Lila about Krav Maga were said to alleviate her worry. He knew he was no match for these men. Unlike Lila, he hadn't realized he would need to be.

"Here we are," Jack called out.

Whatever Sam expected, it wasn't this.

The parking lot of the long, dark green building was empty; a single light over the door cast an almost eerie glow. Not the most welcoming sight.

"Is the place open?"

"Yes and no," Alex said as he put the SUV in park.

Sam slowly unbuckled his seat belt. The other three men were already out of the vehicle, waiting for Sam to join them. He'd asked for this, no backing out now. With a resigned sigh, Sam reached for the door handle.

The cold night air hit his face, bracing after the heated SUV. Jack slapped him on the back.

"Don't look so glum. You aren't going to your execution."

"Is that a promise?"

Jack looked at Alex, then shrugged. "I can almost guarantee it. Damn, it's colder than a witch's tit. Let's get inside."

"I SHOULD HAVE kept my mouth shut," Lila said. She paced the length of her apartment, then turned. The three women and two dogs watched, back and forth, back and forth. Like they were witnessing a one-sided tennis match.

"What were you going to do?" Dani asked. "Hole up here for the entire week? Alex was bound to find out Sam hadn't left town. More than shit would have hit the fan after that."

Lila stopped, her fists clenched in frustration. "Why is it any of his business?"

"That was my question," Tyler said. "It got me a very dirty look."

"Of course, Jack and Drew had to jump in and be all, *we men have to protect our women*." Rose shook her head. "I think they just wanted to be there to cheer Alex on in case a fight breaks out."

"What?"

"Nice going," Dani said to Rose. "Lila, calm down. Do not grab your keys."

"I need to get to Tom Tom's."

Lila headed for the door, and then remembered it was winter. Before she could backtrack to her closet, Dani calmly took the car keys from her hand and led her to the sofa.

"Sit."

"But…"

"Listen," Dani settled her friend. Pouring a glass of wine, she handed it to Lila. "Nothing is going to happen. I made Alex promise he would deliver Sam back to you in the same condition he was in when he left."

"No black eyes? No missing teeth? Sam has great teeth," Lila told the other women. "No caps or veneers. He was born with them."

"I'd be more worried about his balls than his teeth."

"Really?" Dani exclaimed. She turned to Rose. "What is with you tonight? I'm trying to put out a fire. You're trailing behind with a can of gasoline."

"Sorry," Rose said. She grasped Lila's hand. "Dani's right. Alex isn't a hot head. Jack is a born peacemaker. Drew is the wild card. You never can tell what he might do."

"Hey," Tyler exclaimed. "No need to throw my man under the bus." Thinking for a moment, she backtracked. "Okay, I'll give you that one. Drew can be unpredictable, which I love. But he has no reason to go after Sam, or egg Alex on."

"See?" Dani said, patting Lila's hand reassuringly. "Sam will be fine."

As if sensing her distress, Cooper padded over. He put his head on Lila's knee, eager to comfort.

"You understand, don't you?"

Lila put her arms around his neck, burrowing her face into the fur. The big dog seemed to understand they were talking about Sam.

You fell in love him right away, didn't you, boy?

Cooper's big brown eyes seemed to say, "*You, too.*"

Me? No. Lila sighed. *But I'm falling. Hard and fast.*

"I'LL SEE YOUR dollar and raise you two more."

"Somebody's feeling lucky."

"Luck has nothing to do with it. Skill, my friend, nothing but skill."

Sam grinned. The two men exchanging words did so with little heat and obvious affection. Old friends, easy camaraderie. The entire group felt like a laid-back social circle. He had to remind himself these guys met for a reason other than poker. They were a support group. Vets helping vets. He didn't belong. Normally, he would feel out of place. An intruder. Tonight was an exception. They allowed him, Jack, and Drew in because one of their own requested it.

"You're awfully quiet, Sam. I thought you show business types talked all the time."

Sam looked at Tom Unger. He owned *Tom Tom's,* was the group's unofficial leader. It was obvious they looked to him, followed his rules — happily. Be respectful; don't drink too much. Screw up one time too many, don't come back.

"Oh, I can talk your ear off if the situation warrants it," Sam said. He took a sip of beer. "I'm still wondering if I'm here for a talking to or an ass whipping."

"The ass whipping is up to Alex." Tom chuckled. "Don't look so worried. He's a reasonable sort — most of the time. Mess with a man's sister, reason tends to fly out the window."

"I'm not messing with —"

"We're all fond of Lila," Tom interrupted. "She's like one of my own."

Hearing this, the other men at the table chimed in. Lila was either a sister, a daughter, a friend. Steve, new to the group and younger than the rest, let everyone know she was hot. The comment earned him some warning looks and an elbow to the ribs. From Sam.

"Hey," Steve complained. "I didn't say I would ever do anything about it. Isn't a guy allowed to look?"

"Absolutely," Tom told him. "Look, enjoy. Keep your mouth shut. Understood?"

"Understood, Tom."

Impressive. A few softly spoken words, direct eye contact. Tom had the respect of these men. It was genuine, and, if Sam wasn't mistaken, mutual.

"If you ever want a job as my assistant director, let me know. You'd keep everyone in line with a single look."

"I'll keep the offer in mind," Tom said. "Now, let's get down to why you're here tonight."

"Finally," Alex exclaimed. Tom deliberately put the two men on opposite sides of the table. In theory, great. Sam could have done without an evening of dirty looks.

"Alex." Tom's voice was firm. "When you called me to set this up, you agreed to let us take Sam's measure before anything was said or done."

"We've been here two hours, Tom," Alex pointed out. "I've known you to *take a man's measure* in thirty seconds. What's the holdup?"

Unoffended by Alex's outburst, Tom shrugged. "I've made up my mind about Sam. Didn't take long."

"Then —"

Tom held up a hand, instantly silencing Alex.

"I didn't want to influence anyone. You and Lila are family, son."

Sam saw Alex swallow hard when Tom called him son. It seemed the older man was more than a friend; he was a surrogate father. Suddenly this all made sense. If Alex's father were alive, he would consult him. Now, that was Tom's job.

"Sam is a good man," Tom told them. "A little arrogant. Too used to getting his own way," he looked at Alex. "Sound familiar? You met your lady in another country. Her brother was here, blissfully unaware of what was happening."

"I respected Dani," Alex said, a bit defensively.

"I respect Lila." Sam directed his words to Tom. His glanced at Alex, wanting him to understand. "I'll admit this get-together threw me. I've never had a brother, or any family member, worry about a woman I was seeing. Lila is very lucky to have all of you in her life."

"Well said, Sam." Tom looked around the table. Each man nodded. When his eyes stopped on Alex, everyone grew quiet.

"She's my sister," Alex grumbled. There was less heat, more resignation. "Don't hurt her."

"I would rather cut off my left nut."

"Hurt her," Alex told him, "I'll do it for you."

"FINALLY." LILA JUMPED up when she heard the door to the shop open. "I thought they would never get back."

"Four hours," Dani reminded her. "That's about average for poker night."

"Seemed like an eternity."

Lila stopped herself from racing down the stairs. The slightly sick feeling in her stomach grew. The sound of feet on the stairs, more than one pair. One more second, she would scream.

Alex was the first one into the room.

"Don't give me that look," he said. "Loverboy is still in one piece. See?"

Sam looked fine. No visible marks. She started to go to him but her brother's hand on her arm stopped her.

"Nope." He pulled her close, giving her a loving hug. "Big brother first." Alex kissed her cheek, and then whispered, "He was never in any danger."

"I know," she whispered back. Her arms tightened around his waist. She loved him so much. "I was afraid you might stick him on one of Jack and Drew's planes, and then have one of them fly him out of here. Maybe Timbuktu or Kathmandu."

"Mmm, it was a thought." Alex laughed when Lila punched him in the arm. "He's here, isn't he? No harm done."

"Was there any?" Lila asked Sam after everyone left. "Harm done, I mean."

"I'm good. Perfect."

"You've come out of this with your ego intact," Lila laughed. "What went on tonight?"

"Guy stuff," Sam said. He removed his coat and gloves before bending to pet a wiggling Cooper.

"Guy stuff? What? Spitting and cursing and peeing standing up?"

"Pissing."

"I beg your pardon?"

"Guys say piss, not pee." Sam took her in his arms, his grin wide.

"I hate that word; it's… crude."

"My point exactly." He kissed a trail along her jaw. "Men *are* crude. Get a group of us together, and it flows like water. Raunchy jokes. Some bragging over sexual exploits. *Past* sexual exploits. No mention was made of any current relationships."

Lila shook her head in amazement. "Men. Why do you think women are different? We cuss. We tell inappropriate jokes. As for bragging? You wouldn't believe some of the stories I've heard."

"Fair enough." Sam lifted Lila, his arms strong and sure. He headed for the bedroom. "What do you say we give a few more to add to your arsenal?"

Lila didn't tell Sam. Before him, she had no stories. None interesting enough to brag over. By the end of the week, she would. Envy-inducing tales. Lila knew one thing. She would keep the good parts to herself. These moments were *hers*. For the next few days, Sam belonged to her. She wasn't going to share. Not now. Not ever.

SAM QUIETLY LEFT the bed. Watching Lila sleep was a joy. When her eyes were open, she was a constant bundle of beautiful energy. Relaxed, her breathing gentle, she was just as beautiful. This was different. Peaceful. She made his heart —

No. Sam put a screeching halt to those thoughts. His heart was not involved. It couldn't be. Lila belonged in Harper Falls. She had her brother, her friends. He needed the rest of the world. He needed excitement. He craved big cities. New York, London, Los Angeles. His home in Paris. As lovely as Harper Falls was, he knew it wasn't for him. All he had to offer Lila was the occasional visit. She deserved more. She deserved it all. A husband. Children. He wanted all those things too. Someday. But not here. She was planting roots and they were getting deeper every day. Any future for them was impossible.

"Hey, Coop."

Cooper greeted him with a happy smile, his head tipped to the side. Sam would miss him. It hadn't taken long for the dog to worm his way into Sam's affections. A bit like a certain curvy brunette.

"I'm in trouble, Coop," Sam confided to his furry friend. "Promise you'll look after her. I expect you to be a gentleman, keep her company. Keep her safe. Especially keep her safe."

Sam poured himself a glass of water, then filled Cooper's bowl. The sound of the dog lapping up water followed him as he wandered around the room. It was a small living area. Probably too small now that a large dog was added to the mix. They would make do. When she found the right man, they would move to a bigger place.

158

Sam frowned at the thought. He wasn't that man, but picturing Lila with anyone else made his stomach clench. God, he was a selfish bastard. Not that it was a revelation. He was used to having his way — getting what he wanted. He wanted Lila. Couldn't have her. What did he expect? Lila wasn't going into hiding when he left town. Some lucky bastard would snatch her up. He hoped he never heard when it happened.

Lila's desk was neat, like the rest of her apartment. A cordless phone, a laptop. In one corner a spiral notebook with a plain white cover sat. Curious, Sam sat in the chair. He knew this was snooping. The book was closed. That didn't stop him longer than a few seconds. If she wanted to keep the contents private, the drawer was less than a foot away. His reasoning was slightly skewed, but it worked for him. Flipping open the cover, Sam began to read.

Lila stretched her arms above her head. Mmm. The bed was warm, perfect for a cuddle with a big sexy man. To her disappointment, when she reached for Sam, his side was empty. She felt the around. Empty and cold.

Certain he wouldn't have left without telling her, Lila grabbed her robe. The apartment was silent, but there was a faint beam of light under the door. Lila stepped out of the bedroom, searching. When she saw Sam sitting at her desk, reading from her notebook, she started forward. His laughter stopped her in her tracks.

"Which part are you reading?"

Sam's head whipped around, startled.

"Lila," he began. It was too late to feign guilt. It wasn't too late to apologize. "I'm sorry, honey. I know I should have asked first."

"Yes, you should have." She tightened the belt on her robe, and then crossed to join him. "You find my story funny?"

"Funny, sweet, moving. I planned on glancing at it, nothing more. One paragraph and I couldn't put it down."

"I..." she tried to find the words. "Sometimes it's easier to write what I'm feeling."

Sam went to her, clasping her hand in his. So small and delicate. Like Lila.

And like the woman, strong — capable. He gently kissed her cheek.

"The girl in the story. Did you know her?"

"Yes." Lila laid her head on Sam's chest. The beat of his heart both comforting and stirring. "I had a friend in Oregon — my best friend. She lived next door. When she got sick, the cancer moved so fast. I never said goodbye. After all these years, with this story, I'm finally getting to..."

Sam led Lila to the sofa, sitting. He tucked her close, his arm around her.

"The part before, when the girls spy on the brother kissing his girlfriend?"

"That was me," she chuckled.

"The description was priceless. The friend intrigued because of her crush on the older boy. The sister. You. Embarrassed."

"I really made you laugh? You aren't just saying that?"

"You heard me." Sam gave her a straight, clear look. "I didn't know you were there, Lila. But I promise if I had, I wouldn't have laughed to make you feel good."

Lila sighed. "Good. You're the first person to read that story."

"Do you have more?"

"No." Lila shook her head. "Oh, I have some terrible poetry. My angsty teenage phase. In college, I majored in business. My mother encouraged me to take a few creative writing courses. When she died, my desire to write died. Recently, something brought me back to it."

"You're talented, Lila."

Lila's first instinct was to dismiss Sam's compliment. This was her secret, her dream. Having someone feed that dream, especially someone whose opinion she respected, made her uncomfortable. She could hear her mother's encouraging words. The love washed over her. Lila's eyes filled with tears. *Someone else thinks my writing is good, Mom.*

"Hey," Sam said, worry in his eyes. "Why the tears? What I said is a good thing."

"It is," Lila assured him. She hesitated. "Don't laugh."

"Promise."

"I miss my mother."

"Oh, honey." Sam gave her a sweet kiss. "Of course you do."

"She thought I could be a writer, Sam. When you told me I was good, it felt like she was here, wrapping her arms around me. I haven't felt this close to her in years."

Without a word, Sam held her close, letting the gentle tears flow. He felt a tightness in his throat. He couldn't give Lila back her mother. He could help make her dreams come true.

"I know people, Lila."

"We all do, Sam," Lila smiled, her cheeks glistening.

Looking around, Sam found the box of tissues on the coffee table. Grabbing one, he dabbed away her tears.

"*My* people are publishers."

"No."

Lila tried to move away, but Sam held her tight.

"Don't dismiss the idea until you hear me out."

"I don't want my story published."

"But —"

"If I did, I wouldn't want my..." she struggled for the right word. "Whatever you are, using his influence."

"I could get pissed off, fast, at such an accusation." Sam took a deep,

161

calming breath. "You don't know me very well, so let me make something clear. This is my business, Lila. I don't screw around with that. Nepotism, cronyism. I didn't get where I am by putting unqualified, untalented people ahead of more deserving candidates."

"I'm sorry," Lila said, ashamed of herself. "I don't think of myself as a professional writer. It's hard to wrap my head around the idea of being *that* good."

"Well, start."

"This story was never meant to be seen, Sam. Maybe something else. Someday."

"*This*," Sam insisted. "*Now*."

"It's personal," Lila protested. "Who wants to read my ramblings?"

"I do."

"But —"

"Writing about your friend. It's your way of finishing the healing process."

"Yes."

"Think of all the young people dealing with the issue. This story might help." Sam tucked her under his arm, his hand smoothing back her hair. "When *Wishes* came out, the reviews fed my ego. You know what fed my soul? When someone would tell me how much the movie touched them. One lady said she cried for two hours straight then called her mother. They saw it together the next day."

"Did she cry again?"

"They both did," Sam said. "Like babies."

"I don't know, Sam." It was tempting. For so many reasons.

"Think about it. No hurry. No pressure."

"Really?"

Hearing the doubt in her voice, Sam smiled. His reputation for getting what he wanted was well known — and well earned.

"I promise not to push — for now. A month, maybe two, down the road? No guarantees."

Lila felt a rush of emotion that had nothing to with her book. *A month, maybe two, down the road.* A chance to have contact with Sam after this week. Did that make her a glutton for punishment? Getting all tingly thinking about a *chance* to talk with Sam at some unsettled date? Lila didn't care. She would take what she could get and worry about the implications later.

"Deal."

Sam pulled Lila in for a long kiss. He wondered if she realized what she had agreed to. As far as he was concerned, she gave him permission to walk back into her life. As he deepened the kiss, his hands delving under her robe, Sam knew one thing. He wouldn't wait long. A month? He could go without seeing her, touching her, for that long. Then Lila moaned. Her fingers threaded through his hair. The kiss escalated, soared.

"Three weeks," Sam hissed through his teeth when her hand left his hair to cup his erection.

"Hmm?" Lila asked. Her eyes were cloudy with passion.

"Nothing, honey."

Sam lifted Lila. Would his arms feel empty after he left her? Two weeks would be pushing his luck. Three. Definitely three.

CHAPTER SIX

THE WEEK FLEW by. Time never dragged when you wanted it to.

Lila felt like she was in a strange bubble. Insulated from the outside world, yet aware that as every minute passed, their time together slipped away.

With the holiday rush behind her, she could leave *Peony* in the hands of her very competent assistant manager. Lila was free to spend her days, and nights, playing with Sam.

Alex and her friends left them in peace. No unannounced visits or off-hours phone calls. She was in touch, in a normal way; as though she didn't have a temporary roommate whom everyone knew shared her bed. She knew Alex wasn't happy with the situation, but she appreciated his backing off. He let her make her own decisions. He acknowledged she was an adult. Lila loved him all the more for it.

They took Cooper for long walks. They found he was a snow dog, happy to frolic for hours. He would chase anything that moved, squirrel, leaf. It was all fair game. Being outdoors with his two favorite people, Cooper was in doggy heaven.

When they returned to the apartment, Cooper collapsed in an exhausted heap, content, and ready to sleep for hours. Lila and Sam used the time to become better acquainted. They would share a quiet meal, discussing a wide variety of topics. Nothing was out of bounds. Politics, religion. Global warming, pollution. *Family Guy* versus *American Dad*. They agreed on most subjects, debated others with a heated respectfulness.

Either way, it always ended the same — in bed. Or on the couch. On the floor. In the shower. The sex was sometimes playful. Sometimes intense. Always satisfying beyond her wildest imagination. Sam was a dream lover. Considerate, inventive, and willing to let Lila experiment. Even when her fantasy turned out to be completely impractical.

"Where did you hear about this position?"

"In a book."

"Not *The Joy of Sex*?" Sam tried to adjust his position. Logistically, Tab A was not going to fit into Slot B.

"No."

Lila shifted. She peered up at him between her spread legs. Bent over, grasping her ankles was an incredibly awkward sex position. Not to mention uncomfortable.

"The *Kama Sutra*?"

"*My Wild Weekend with the Billionaire Next Door.*"

"Ah."

Giving up, Lila straightened. Her only consolation was she could blame her red face on her head being upside down instead of embarrassment. If she was honest, the two were equally to blame.

"Do you often let dubious romance novels guide your sex play?"

"This was the first time," Lila admitted. When Sam began to laugh, she gave him a dirty look. "Hey, it worked for Lance and Angelique."

"Honey, those names alone should give you pause. Lance? As in, his lance thrust into her pleasure hole?"

Lila lost it. She collapsed onto the sofa in a fit of giggles. It wasn't just the words; it was who said them. Sam Laughton, big, bad entertainment mogul spewing horribly dated romance novel euphemisms. If they weren't naked, she would have wished for a camera.

"You need to get with the times, my friend. These days, authors call a spade a spade. Or in this case, a cock a cock."

"Maybe," Sam conceded. "But Lance? Come on."

Hours later, lying in Sam's arms, Lila smiled. He could be so silly. Making her laugh in unexpected ways. Then, on the turn of a dime, he became a focused, passionate lover. At those times, she felt they were the only two people in the world — that she was the only woman he could ever want with such single-minded intensity. If she saw something that wasn't there, she didn't want to know. For the next day and a half, Sam was hers. When he left? Lila mentally shrugged. She refused to miss him before he was gone.

"I can almost hear your mind working," Sam whispered. He nuzzled the side of her neck. "I thought I wore you out. What has you awake when you should be resting up for our next mind-blowing sexual escapades?"

I'm going to miss you. I can't begin to comprehend how much. You've become important. Too important. Who will I talk to late at night? Whose silly jokes will I laugh at? Who will make love to me with white-hot passion, and then hold me as if I'm made of spun glass? And how can I tell you any of this? The answer was simple. She couldn't.

"Lila? Honey? Is something wrong?"

"Yes." Lila wound her arms around Sam's neck. "It's been a whole fifteen minutes since you kissed me."

Sam knew there was more to it. Her tense shoulders, the sadness in her eyes. But he let it go — didn't push. For Lila's sake. And his own.

"A whole fifteen minutes?" Sam rolled her underneath him. "How have you survived?"

Good question, Lila thought. She lifted her mouth, taking Sam's kiss. Savoring. *How would she survive?*

"HELLO, STRANGER. I was wondering if I would see you before you left town."

Sam smiled. Rose yelled the words as she hurried across the street. He took the overflowing canvas bags from her hands.

"Did you cancel tonight's party?"

"No," Rose said. She gave him a friendly kiss on the cheek, efficiently rubbing away the dab of lipstick she'd left behind. "Those bags are full of last minute party necessities. I thought you and Lila might opt out. Word around town is you only venture out to walk the dog."

"Are people saying nasty things about Lila?"

"Of course not," Rose laughed. "She is universally adored. You're both legal and single. The men are jealous. The women are envious. Why would you think otherwise?"

"Harper Falls is a small town."

"Peyton Place." Rose smiled. "You need to update your reading material, Sam."

"That's the second time in the past day someone's told me that."

"Sounds like a story."

Sam shook his head. "A private one."

"Those are the best kind." Rose hooked her arm through his. "Where is the

166

lady in question?"

"She had a shipping snafu to wade through." Sam escorted Rose to her car. "She's meeting me in a few minutes for lunch."

"Any chance you'll be sticking around after tomorrow?"

"No," Sam said firmly. He loaded her bags into the trunk. "Why would you ask?"

"You changed your plans once."

"Rearranged, not changed," Sam corrected. "This is my vacation time. I simply chose to spend it all in Harper Falls."

"With Lila."

"Are you trying to be subtle, Rose?"

"A little," she admitted sheepishly.

"Well, you're lousy at it. If there's something you want to ask, spit it out."

"Okay. Remember you asked for it."

Sam didn't like the glint in Rose's eyes.

"Can I change my mind?"

Rose shook her head. "I only have one question. Are you going to break Lila's heart?"

"Shit."

"I'll take that as a yes."

The condemnation was what set him off. Under normal circumstances, Sam would have easily brushed off Rose's comment. These circumstances were anything *but* normal.

"What about my heart?" he threw out. There was plenty of heat behind his words. Enough to make Rose's eyes widen with surprise.

"I never thought about it."

"Why would you? I'm experienced. Worldly. Lila is sweet. A forgettable Christmas fling."

"Sam —"

"Lila is *not* forgettable, Rose." Frustrated, Sam ran a hand through his hair. "She's bright, funny, beautiful — sexy as hell. I like her. I…"

"You're in love with her," Rose finished for him.

"Is that so hard to believe?"

"Yes."

"I don't know who you're insulting. Me, or Lila."

"You know what I mean, Sam," Rose said. "You are a player. With a big, fat capital P. Admit it, you're as surprised as I am by this turn of events."

Sam couldn't argue.

"Lila is… a revelation." The reverence in his voice was so poignant it brought tears to Rose's eyes.

"Sam Laughton. Who knew you had the soul of a poet." Rose sighed, happy for both her friends. "When are you going to ask her to marry you?"

"I'm not."

"Alex won't like it." Rose shrugged. "Dani will bring him around. A few months without a ring on her finger won't make a difference."

"You don't understand, Rose. I'm not asking her to marry me. Not now. Not ever." Sam cleared his throat. The lump wouldn't move. He was afraid it never would. "When I leave, that's it. I thought I might keep in touch. Visit. But I know that would be a mistake. For both of us."

"Sam." Rose didn't like the look of despair she saw on his face. He stopped at nothing to get what he wanted. Lila loved him, Rose was certain. Why was he walking away from a sure thing?

"It's cold out here, Rose. Go home. I'll see you tonight."

"I'm not budging until you explain this idiocy."

"This is Lila's home, Rose. When she lost her parents, she was drifting — alone." Sam's heart ached when he thought of the tears she shed when she shared her grief. "She has so much here in Harper Falls. A successful business, friends. And most important, her brother. She needs him. She needs all of you. I can't ask her to give it up."

"You picked a hell of a time to get selfless, Sam."

"I've never been in love before."

Rose watched Sam walk away. Love was supposed to be glorious. More often than not, it was just plain hard.

168

"HAPPY NEW YEAR, Lila."

Lila hugged her brother, grateful once again to have him here. Too many times, she rang in another year with no idea of his whereabouts, or his safety. Knowing that was a thing of the past, helped ease some of the pain she felt. She no longer counted the days until Sam left. Now it was hours and minutes.

"I can still beat the shit out of him for you."

Lila let out a small chuckle. "Sam didn't make me any promises, Alex. I went into this with my eyes wide open."

"I did the same thing when I met Dani." Alex looked across the room at the woman who owned his heart. "I fell in love, knowing I shouldn't. Five years didn't change a damn thing. The second I saw her it could have been five minutes. And I'm an idiot."

"I'm not going to cry," Lila assured her brother. However, it was a close thing. "You don't have to worry about me." Then she did something she had never done before; she lied to her brother's face. "This is a crush, not love. I'll miss Sam for a little while. In a few weeks, he'll be nothing more than a happy memory."

Lila knew Alex didn't believe her. She thought for a moment that he would push her. Thankfully, he let it go. Seeing Sam hold up a glass of champagne, a welcoming smile on his face. Lila willed an answering smile. By the time she reached Sam, she wasn't faking. This was New Year's Eve. A time to celebrate, not mourn.

Wrapping her arms around Sam's neck, Lila gave him a long passionate kiss. They still had a few hours, and she planned on making the most of every second.

"YOU LUCKED OUT on the weather. They're predicting a big snowstorm for tomorrow. Today is clear as a bell."

Lila hated that she was reduced to making small talk. *The weather*? Right now, it was just sad. One more inane comment would topple over into pathetic. It would be nice if Sam would help her out. For the last half hour, his contribution to the conversation amounted to a few grunts followed by the occasional, mmhmm. Was he that anxious to leave that he couldn't be bothered to use actual words?

Lila couldn't complain about their last night together. Cooper was having a sleepover at Rose and Jack's house, so there was no dog to walk. They fell into bed, unable to get enough of each other. So many emotions passed between them. Desperation. Tenderness. The underlying wistfulness couldn't temper the passion or the need to pack as much as possible into these last few precious hours.

Now, with Sam's departure imminent, Lila felt like she watched a stranger pack his bag.

"What are your plans when you get to Los Angeles?"

"Work."

"I know." Lila wanted to shout the words. Instead, she kept her tone light and friendly. "Is there anything specific? We haven't talked about your next project. Is it a movie?"

"Does it matter?"

"Sam. Any second now, I'm going to hit you over the head with the nearest heavy object. Not only will that delay your trip, but I'll be left with a huge mess. Do you know how hard it will be to get blood out of the rug you're standing on?"

When he didn't answer, Lila temper blew.

"Fine. At least do me a favor and move to the right. The kitchen tile is easier to clean."

Lila spun away, tears welling in her eyes. Stupid, stupid man.

"Marry me, Lila."

Sam heard her gasp. She didn't speak or turn. He couldn't see the expression on her face. He was flying blind. After the way he'd acted all morning, it was probably what he deserved.

Neither he nor Lila had a second of sleep the night before. They made the most of every moment. If they weren't making love, they were holding on, pretending the seconds weren't ticking away.

They took one last shower. Came together one more time. Then Sam's brain started working overtime. He heard Lila. He knew she was trying to keep things light. All the time, he was having an argument with himself.

Why couldn't he have Lila? He knew she loved him. She might not see her brother every day, but they could visit. The rest could be worked out later. They belonged together. That was all that mattered.

Blurting out a marriage proposal wasn't the smoothest move he'd ever made, but there it was. As the seconds ticked by, he began to wonder if he'd made a huge miscalculation. Maybe this wasn't what Lila wanted.

"Lila, I know this seems sudden."

"No."

Sam frowned. "No, this isn't sudden?"

"No, I won't marry you."

Sam watched as she turned, stunned to see a huge smile on her face. His world was crumbling around him and she was smiling?

"I see," Sam said stiffly.

"We can't get married, or engaged. Not after a week. When we know each other better, ask me again." She thought for a moment. "On Valentine's day. I'll say yes."

Sam swooped Lila into his arms, twirling her around and around until they were both laughing and breathless.

"Wait." Sam pulled back before he could seal it with a kiss. "I have to leave, Lila. There are meetings — business I can't postpone. How are we supposed to get to know each other when we aren't in the same zip code?"

"Tell me you love me."

"Lila."

"Say it, and then I will answer your question."

Sam put his hand under her chin, gently lifting until her eyes met his. His clear blue eyes told her everything. But she still wanted the words.

"I love you, Lila. I know it's been fast, but that doesn't make it any less true. If you'll give me the chance, I will spend every day, for the rest of my life, showing you."

"I swore if the man of my dreams ever told me he loved me, I wouldn't cry." She wiped at the tears on her cheeks. "Just goes to show, you can't plan these things."

"Hey," Sam said, kissing her lightly. "Isn't there something you need to tell me?"

"Right. About our logistics problem."

"Lila."

She loved the way he said her name when he was exasperated. Or when he was happy, or making love with her. She loved everything about him.

"I love you, Sam. A long-distance relationship doesn't cut it for me. So, like it or not, Cooper and I are going with you. Today."

Sam wasn't going to argue. It was exactly what he wanted. He did have a few pertinent questions.

"The shop? Are you okay with leaving *Peony*? Trusting someone else to run your baby?"

"*Peony* has kept me busy, but it isn't my passion or my dream. I want to be a writer, Sam. I want my story published. *If* your contacts think it's good enough."

"I promise to leave the decision in their hands."

What he didn't tell her was his certainty the book would be published. Without any push from him. It was that good. He'd bet anything there would be a bidding war. The sky was the limit. That was something Lila would have the pleasure of finding out when the time came. He wasn't going to spoil the surprise.

"And your brother? Your friends?"

"I will miss seeing them all the time." Lila relaxed in his arms. "Alex will understand. Everyone else will be happy for me. For us."

"Then what are we waiting for?" Sam pushed Lila towards her closet. "Pack your bags, my love. We have a dog to pick up."

EPILOGUE

LILA'S EYES FLEW open. Eight o'clock? Why was she still in bed on the most important day of her life? Then she remembered. On the night *before* the most important day of her life, Sam did some very creative things with his mouth and a feather duster.

Lila sighed. She floated on a happiness high. One that started on New Year's Day and hadn't waned. Six weeks. A private jet to Los Angeles. Sam's meetings kept them there for several days. Then New York. Broadway, late night suppers. Exclusive designer boutiques — with the *actual* designer present. Finally, Paris. Home.

Lila threw back the covers. A shower in the luxurious bathroom was what she needed. She slipped from the bed, pausing at the window. The neighborhood was one of the most exclusive in Paris. They were somewhere over the Atlantic Ocean when Sam mentioned the location of his apartment. Saint Germain-des-Prés. Lila quickly looked it up. Holy crap.

"Sam?" Lila asked in a hushed tone.

"Yes?"

Sam, reclining in one of the plane's cushy chairs, put the script he was reading on a pile of six or seven others. Potential future projects. Though nothing was catching his interest.

Lila's eyes were as wide as saucers. Through this entire whirlwind, she tried to maintain an even keel. Impressed, but not gushing. She didn't want Sam to think he'd saddled himself with an unsophisticated twit. This was too much. How could you maintain a blasé attitude when your future home was not only in Paris but on the Seine?

"Do you know where you live?"

"Where *we* live," Sam corrected. "And yes, I'm acquainted with the area."

"Oscar Wilde and Cole Porter lived there." Lila bounced up, bursting with excitement. "Paris, Sam. I'm in love and going to live in Paris."

"Finally." Sam snagged Lila around the waist, pulling her onto his lap. "I was wondering what it would take to strip away that ridiculous veneer of sophistication you put up."

"You knew I was faking?" Lila frowned. "Why didn't you say anything?"

"Honey." Sam kissed her cheek. "Everything happened so fast. If you needed to put on a temporary mask out in public while you adjusted, I was fine with that. As long as you were you in private, I had no complaints."

"I was afraid if I ran around all wide-eyed, asking questions. Pointing at one thing after another, you might dump me back in Harper Falls and find yourself a woman less inclined to gawk."

"Never again," Sam said sternly. "Don't hide yourself from me, Lila. I love your enthusiasm. I'm looking forward to showing you Paris. I want to see it again for the first time with you — through your eyes."

"Be careful what you ask for," Lila warned. She relaxed, perhaps for the first time since leaving Harper Falls. "I want to see everything."

And that's what she did. When Sam wasn't working, he walked with her. The rest of the time, Lila was happy to wander Paris on her own. It would take years, decades, to see it all. She could hardly wait.

After a quick shower, Lila threw on a pair of jeans, a burgundy sweater, and thick socks. Paris in February was damp and chilly. Then she went looking for her men.

"Sam? Cooper?"

No response. Maybe they were out for their morning run. Cooper was adjusting to his new lifestyle beautifully. You would think he was born to city life. Maybe he was? They didn't know. But he belonged to them now, and they belonged to him. She, Sam, and Cooper. A very happy family.

Smelling coffee, Lila walked to the kitchen. Sam enlarged the area before he moved in. He managed to keep the Parisian feel while updating it to fit his modern tastes. She reached for a mug when she heard the front door open.

"Hey," she called out. "I was wondering where you were."

Lila looked in the living room, a smile of greeting on her face. Cooper sat alone in the middle of the room, smiling back.

"I know you're talented, but you did not come in by yourself."

Lila knelt, patting Cooper's head. Suddenly, she noticed the red, silk ribbon tied around his neck.

"What's this?"

Making a closer examination, Lila ran her hand over the ribbon. She froze when she felt the circle of metal. A ring.

"It's Valentine's Day."

"That's what the calendar says."

Sam. Lila's heart skipped a beat. She couldn't believe he was hers. Gorgeous, sexy. Blue eyes to die for. Kind. Not perfect, but perfect for her.

Sam took the ribbon, letting the ring fall into his hand.

"I know you better than I did six weeks ago," he began. "I hope to spend the rest of my life growing with you, changing. Doing my best to make you happy. Loving you. Marry me, Lila. Please?"

Sam Laughton. The man helped her make her dreams come true. What else could she say?

"Yes."

www.ingramcontent.com/pod-product-compliance
Lightning Source LLC
Chambersburg PA
CBHW060818120626
46557CB00001B/272